CAMPGROUND
CHRONICLES

CAMPGROUND CHRONICLES

Short Stories 1-3

Carol Evans

Copyright

Campground Chronicles: Short Stories 1-3, second edition paperback (ISBN No. 978-1-7339968-1-5) and ebook (Amazon ASIN No. B081143468), copyright © 2019.

Second editions include minor changes to the first edition individual stories.

Billy: A Campground Chronicles Short Story (No. 1), 1st edition ebook, copyright © 2016.

Lucy: A Campground Chronicles Short Story (No. 2), 1st edition ebook, copyright © 2017.

Sassy: A Campground Chronicles Short Story (No. 3), 1st edition ebook, copyright © 2019.

Disclaimer

Fact and Fiction

Slices of truth, like slices of pie, are best dished out in moderation.

Billy is the only one of the three stories contained in this volume that is a true story. The events transpired while the author worked as a camp host in Tennessee during the summer of 2016. The author exercised creative license when filling in the blanks for things she did not directly witness, and she changed the timing of some events. She tried to keep her interpretation of others' thoughts, feelings, and motives to a minimum, leaving most of that to the reader.

While **Lucy** and **Sassy** are fictitious tales, they both draw heavily upon the author's life experiences and relationships, seasoned with a large helping of imagination, and sprinkled with little bits of love.

Where necessary, names in all three stories have been changed to respect the privacy of any real people involved... and because the author has always loved the name Lucy.

Contents

Dedication

Billy is dedicated to the real-life Billy. I hope and pray that life has treated him and his family well since our encounter.

Lucy is dedicated to my son, Sam. He suggested I write a story about my childhood to help break my writer's block. I can't really do a straightforward story like that. This sideways version slipped out instead. I am and ever will be grateful to him for encouraging me to continue writing, for his comments on the draft story, and for the hope he gives me that love, indeed, never dies.

Sassy is dedicated to my faithful friend of 14 years, Dawny Virgil Prewash Sassy Generous Evans (aka the Midnight Unicorn); to my new buddy, Boo; and to all of those faithful, four-legged friends who bless our lives. Special appreciation also goes to Joyce, who adorned Dawny with her fourth (and best suited) name, Sassy. To Ann W., who ensured that the Midnight Unicorn had the time of her life during our visit to her home. And to Carol and John, who exemplify the best of Texas hospitality, and who loved Dawny almost as much as they seem to love me.

BILLY

A Campground Chronicles
Short Story (No. 1)

The heart of this story rings true,
through and through
Echoes on the edges, a reader's imagination
The rest takes shape in the mist in between
which
I suspect
carries more truth than not

Two Tires!

"LOOK!" the young man yelled, running up to Lucy as she approached his family's campsite. "Look! Look at what happened to our tire!"

He waved a shredded loop of rubber in the air and pointed to the mismatched, small tire on the family's double-axle, beat up, open-bed trailer.

"We had *two* tires blow out on our way here!" The delight in his voice and on his face contrasted sharply to the exhausted demeanor of the man Lucy assumed to be the father, who was trying to find his driver's license number for the check-in records.

Backing away from the young man's exuberance and edging closer to the father, Lucy asked, "And how many people will be on the site?"

He had to think about that. He looked around and counted the heads wandering about the trailer, slowly untying the load to set up camp. Lucy wondered how a parent could not immediately know how many children they had with them. He had to start over a couple of times before settling on an estimate of eight, excluding anyone under four-feet tall.

"Can I pet your dog?" the young man interrupted, making a beeline for Sassy, hand outstretched and ready to make contact regardless of Lucy's answer.

Scooting a few steps back and out of reach, she quickly responded, "No, thank you. She's on duty with me and shouldn't be petted."

In reality, Lucy wasn't too sure how Sassy, her aging canine sidekick, would react to the young man's unbridled energy. She had trouble with it herself.

"Billy." The man's calm but firm voice got the boy's immediate attention. "Go help unpack."

Billy looked crestfallen at Sassy's second-hand rejection and left his father and Lucy to finish the check-in process. Included in the exchange of information, the father softly mentioned that one of the kids was bipolar and autistic. Then he mumbled something about ADHD. Lucy couldn't tell if he was referring to one or more or which of the children.

By the time Lucy turned to leave, Billy had fully recovered. "Look!" he yelled, holding out a deck of cards.

"Yes, yes, very nice," she said, carefully backing up to the road. Continuing her dog walk patrol, Lucy could hear Billy going on and on and on about this and that and the other.

His was the last voice to fade away under the evening crescendo of cricket song.

One Handbasket

Lucy had signed up for five months of camp hosting at this small, southern state park. She was nervous about such a long commitment, but it was a charming location and a great place to enjoy her daily walks with Sassy. She ranked campgrounds on a number of factors, the most important being the quality of dog walks available.

Lucy and Sassy had been on the road for two years, living and traveling in their 25-foot motorhome. In the lingo of the RV community, she was a full-timer. Her house, car, doghouse, entry foyer, gourmet kitchen, entertainment center, office, spa, lounge—everything you could want—traveled with her and Sassy in their 400 square-foot house on wheels.

It had been a dream of Lucy's since she was a young girl to travel the country like this. She also wanted to be a writer, so she wrote a blog, using it to journal her travels and experiences. The blog was a great place to express herself, practice her writing, and pretend she had someone to talk to other than the dog.

To keep expenses down, Lucy signed up for camp host jobs wherever possible, getting a free campsite in exchange for labor. Lucy had a tight budget and, being a disciplined, organized sort of gal, kept careful track of all expenditures. She took great delight in her budget's bottom line during those months she was able to camp host.

In this park, Lucy was one of four hosts running the campground. Teamwork could be dicey business if there was any conflict between the members, but this team worked together seamlessly and became fast friends. Lucy grew especially close to Laura, a young woman full-timing with her husband, their daughter, a cat, and a dog. Now that was a full house on wheels!

For the most part, the campers who visited the park were delightful. Many came from the local area, from nearby farms and small towns. Some of them had been coming there for decades, enjoying the campground as their vacation home-away-from-home.

Lucy managed to learn the computer reservation system and other administrative procedures just fine. But dealing with people—their complaints and, worse, the hostility some of them displayed when notified of rule infractions—was a very stressful part of her job. Not only was Lucy an off-the-charts introvert, she detested confrontation.

Sure, the rangers were in the park during working hours and could be called upon to help when needed. But their office was a fair distance from the campground, and they were usually focusing their attention elsewhere in the park.

This left the hosts holding the front line, interfacing with the campers from the time they checked in until the time they left. It was the camp host's door that took the midnight knock if someone wanted to report a loud, obnoxious neighbor. The camp host was the first to check the situation out before calling in a ranger. By the time a ranger actually arrived, especially after-hours, things could conceivably travel quite a distance towards hell in a handbasket.

A Grandma

"GRANDMA!!!"

The poor woman screamed and nearly jumped out of her skin. It was dark. It was late. She was tent camping alone. Billy had come up behind her while she was digging around in the back of her car to retrieve something for her tent.

"Grandma!" he yelled again, his open arms and total delight doing nothing, absolutely nothing to mitigate the poor woman's terror. Billy was 18 years old and about six feet tall.

Totally shaken, the woman knocked on the camp host's door that night to report what had happened. First thing in the morning, she moved to a different site—as far away from Billy's as possible. Lucy was relieved she hadn't been on duty that night.

The rangers had a talk with the family the next day. Billy said he was sorry, but he thought the woman's car looked like his grandmother's and that she had come to visit. He had been so excited.

Indeed.

Spam

Though she loved her roaming lifestyle, Lucy struggled with dark moods. A doctor prescribed anti-depressants for her once, but she didn't take them long. After reading the warning booklet that accompanied the pills, she found that, because the medication was hard on the liver, you weren't supposed to drink alcohol while taking it.

She tossed the pills and poured a glass of wine.

Lucy also loved traveling solo, with Sassy serving as copilot and invaluable companion. But, while she had made some really good friends along the way, there were times she felt something lacking... some depth of human touch.

She knew she was in the dumps when she started seeking emotional validation from the spam comments that came into her blog. Before deleting them, she always skimmed through. There were some real gems:

"Oh my goodness! Incredible article dude!" That drew a smile every time she saw it, which was at least weekly.

"Hello! I love your writing very much! Looking forward to peer you." That was just creepy.

"Excellent website... I'm sending it to several friends and also sharing in delicious. And, obviously, thanks for your sweat!" Put that into the beyond creepy file.

"My brother suggested I may like this blog. He used to be totally right." Was that a backhanded insult to the brother or to her? Probably both.

"Good mechanics and shops are hard to come by these days." Lucy couldn't agree more.

"Very soon this website will be famous amid all blog people, due to its fastidious articles or reviews." Blog people... hmmm... Lucy wondered if they were related to *bog* people and pictured greenish-purple bipedal blobs struggling out of the muck of the internet swamp.

"The object of the game is to breed and raise several dragons for gold."

Yes, well. Sometimes it just didn't matter that some illiterate huckster spammed the same ridiculous comment out to thousands of blogs without reading a word. Lucy took her smiles wherever she could find them, then hung on for dear life—dragons and bog people be damned.

A Smile

Billy pulled a reluctant grin out of Lucy the next morning. She ran into him coming out of the men's room, his straw-colored hair sticking up like the bristles of a whisk broom.

"He-eeey! Look!" He proudly pointed to his head. "I used the hot air hand dryer in the bathroom to dry my hair. I'm gonna do this every day!"

Bog People

Lucy was on duty, so her site was listed on the campground office window in case anyone needed help after hours.

She felt badly for the poor lady who knocked on her door that night. The fan was set on high and she was sleeping the sleep of the grateful dead. She heard nothing until Sassy's alarm bark woke her to the tiny tapping on their door.

Traveling alone, even with an incredible, protective sidekick like Sassy, Lucy didn't feel comfortable opening her door after dark unless she could see and recognize the person outside as non-threatening.

So, here was this lovely lady—who probably came over instead of her husband so that Lucy would *not* feel threatened—standing outside trying to whisper information about some noisy children through the crack Lucy had opened in her kitchen window.

Campers don't want to aggravate troublemakers any more than camp hosts do. The possibility of retaliation can be nerve-racking in a part of the country where nearly everyone carries a gun and a fair portion of those carry hair-trigger tempers. Lucy and Laura shared the concern that some disgruntled camper might vandalize their rigs one day because they resented being reported for a rule infraction. Even tactfully reminding a camper of a rule often drew a defensive retort.

Lucy got enough of the gist of what the lady was saying to know that she needed to go out to talk to her and investigate the problem. She threw on her clothes and, without thinking, turned on the outside light. Opening the door, the light and Sassy's outrageous barking blasted into the night, ensuring that Lucy and her visitor were no longer having a private conversation.

After talking a little more with the lady, Lucy trudged over to the sandbox to round up half a dozen or so rowdy kids, ranging in age from five or six to young teens. She recognized some of them as troublemakers from earlier in the day, but she wasn't sure what site they belonged to.

Off to the side, she spotted an older girl with a cell phone plastered to her ear. Pegging her as the one "in charge," Lucy asked her to take her to their site. The girl rolled her eyes, mumbled something into her phone, and complied. The gaggle of bog-monster children followed.

Upon their arrival, Lucy was met by hostile glares from the group of adults lounging around their campfire. One scrawny man stood up and approached her.

"It's after quiet time and the children are making too much noise." Lucy addressed the man in what she hoped was a firm but respectful tone.

"We didn't hear anything," he shot back. His look dripped venom.

"I could hear them," Lucy responded, not wanting to create any issues for the camper who had complained. "Please keep the kids on your site now and keep them quiet."

"There's no rule about them having to be on the site," he snarled.

"I'll be happy to call the ranger and he can discuss it with you," Lucy replied. It was an empty threat, since the ranger on duty that night lived about an hour away from the park.

"How 'bout if I go over there with them?" the man pressed.

Knowing full well he was baiting her, Lucy cut the conversation short.

"No, thank you," she snapped, and she turned and walked away, wondering why she had said *that*. It seemed a pretty lame response, but it was all she had. Fortunately, it got her out of there before things escalated.

Nevertheless, in the days that followed until those campers left, Lucy felt exposed and vulnerable. After they left, they complained to the state park headquarters about the mean camp hosts.

"I hate people I hate people I hate people..."

It did not bode well when Lucy reached the point where that became her mantra. There were days when she was so drained, she wasn't sure she would be able to complete the five months she had promised.

Boundaries

Billy's family had been around for almost a week before Lucy began to sort out how many kids they had. In the category of under four-feet tall, there was one baby, one toddler, and a girl about six years old.

In addition to Billy, the older kids included five other teenagers/young adults. Two boys and three girls. She wasn't sure if the older ones were all siblings. They seemed awfully close in age to one another to be siblings.

She did discover that the father was Billy's stepdad when Billy corrected her one day after she called him his father. She speculated that the younger kids were the stepdad and mother's offspring, and that the older ones belonged somehow to the mother.

In contrast to Billy and the younger kids, the other older ones were really skinny and quiet. They were very respectful when they needed to interact with someone (buying ice, borrowing the campground horseshoes, etc.), but they gave little opening for small talk or questions. Whenever Lucy saw any of them going to the bathhouse, they did not take shortcuts across other people's sites. They stayed on the road, unlike 90 percent of the other kids and adults in the campground. That small act spoke volumes.

Lucy never learned any of the other older kids' names. With rare exception, they kept to themselves, hovering in the background and along the sidelines. They were nearly invisible compared to Billy, painting a muted canvas behind Billy's bright antics.

Meanwhile, Billy had no compunction about traipsing across sites, approaching fellow campers with his open smile and cheerful greeting. He would settle into a camp chair, put his feet up on the picnic table, and visit away as long as they would let him or until something drew his attention elsewhere. A couple of times he tried to enter someone's rig uninvited as if he were just another member of the family.

Finally, Lucy started telling anyone pulling into the section near Billy's site that there was a gregarious young man nearby and if they did not want him to visit or wanted him to leave, to just say so clearly, and he would listen. She reassured them that he was harmless, but that they needed to be firm if they wanted him to hear them. She was trying to help them to set boundaries. Lucy was an expert at that.

Billy, on the other hand, had no boundaries. Once he made an acquaintance, the next time he saw them, his arms would open wide for a hug.

"I don't do hugs," Lucy blurted out the first time he came at her with open arms. He only asked once.

He may have been disappointed, but he certainly didn't hold it against her, for he never missed a chance to yell out his sing-song "HE-EEEY!!!" across the campground if she was remotely within earshot.

Colors

Other than Billy's boundless ways that caused a fair amount of upset and distress, the rest of his clan caused no trouble. Unless you counted the parents, who often left Billy and an assortment of other children behind all day and sometimes well into the night while they went off somewhere unknown, leaving the camp hosts to deal with any repercussions.

One day, one of Billy's older brothers kindly unloaded wood from the back of the work cart for Lucy when she drove up to deliver it to their neighbor. She and the neighbor had been chatting, and by the time she turned around to offload the wood, the young man had wordlessly taken care of it. He simply continued on his way to the bathhouse before she even had a chance to thank him.

The next day, he approached Lucy while she and Sassy were on their morning walk.

"Good morning," he softly greeted her. "I like your dog."

"Thank you," Lucy replied, surprised to hear the young man speak for the first time. He had a slow and gentle voice.

"I was wondering what it takes to be a lifeguard here. I know how to be a lifeguard. I've done it before." He looked at her hopefully.

"Oh, you'll need to check with the rangers at the main office about that," Lucy responded.

"I did," he admitted. "They said they didn't need anyone right now."

He nodded at Lucy politely, smiled at Sassy, and continued on his way back to his site.

Lucy could tell he really wanted to work.

But the family only had the one truck. And the mother and father and younger children were usually away in it during the day. Working somewhere, or looking for work, Lucy imagined.

Imagine.

How often, she wondered later that evening, do people imagine themselves in someone else's shoes? Walking their path? Seeing the world in the colors they see? Do they see the world in black and white, screaming for judgment and criticism? Is it bleak and gray, filled with countless challenges, both of their own making and not? Or is it painted in colors of their own choosing, should they be so lucky to have a choice and the initiative, the courage... the opportunity to make that choice?

Doesn't everybody have a choice?

No. Not always. Not about everything.

Lucy finished her wine and went to bed.

Burgers

Lucy was working at her computer one evening when she noticed Billy making himself at home at her neighbor's. He lounged at their picnic table, his bare feet propped on the bench, while the woman grilled burgers for herself and her daughters.

As she had done on many occasions with other campers by this time, Lucy approached and asked how everything was going.

"Just fine," her neighbor reassured her. "Billy is welcome to visit for a while. It's not the first time," she smiled sweetly.

"Ok, sounds good," replied Lucy. Addressing Billy, she continued. "Be sure to leave when you are asked to do so. Remember, this is their site and you need to respect that."

"No problem!" he responded with a big grin.

Lucy returned to her rig, occasionally looking out the window to watch Billy's animated ways while her neighbor worked on her family's dinner.

And that is when she noticed one of Billy's sisters standing a few feet from the picnic table. She wasn't interacting with Billy or the neighbor. She was simply staring at and fiddling with her phone. It struck Lucy how unusual it was for her—or any of the other children—to be around Billy when he was off on one of his jaunts.

When Lucy's neighbor told Billy that it was time to leave, his sister quietly followed.

No problem.

No burgers, either.

It started to sink in how extraordinarily thin those older kids were. Billy, on the other hand, had a much healthier build. Lucy didn't directly see it until later, but she guessed he was able to partake of quite a few snacks during his rounds. Probably even snag a meal or two. Hopefully, with some to spare.

A Ninja

Things came to a head the following weekend. The campground was filled to the max. There was no way the camp hosts could keep track of everything Billy was up to or run interference before he became a bother.

Late on Friday night, a group of campers were relaxing and visiting around their fire a few sites down from Billy's. Billy crept up behind one of the men, put his hands on the man's shoulders and, in an eerie voice announced, "Don't mock me. Be nice or I will come back later tonight dressed as a ninja!"

The next day, the man lodged a complaint that they felt threatened by Billy. He demanded the campground do something.

After talks between the rangers and Billy's parents, Billy was restricted to his site unless accompanied by a parent.

The mother was very unhappy with that decision. Lucy overheard her complain to the father the next morning. "They just don't get Billy. Nobody else has any problems with him."

"Let's move to another county!" Billy interjected.

That afternoon, two of Billy's sisters approached Lucy to speak about his banishment.

"He is 18, but he has the mind of an eight-year old," said the one.

"He would never hurt somebody," stressed the other.

It was the most Lucy heard the girls speak the entire time of their visit, as if they had finally found their voices now that Billy's was somewhat quieted. And it was obvious that they cared very much for their brother.

On Sunday morning, as was typical, two-thirds of the campers left. As Lucy and Sassy walked down the road behind Billy's site, he gleefully greeted her. "He-eeey! Guess what!

Those people that lied about me left and now I can go anywhere I want to again!"

"Oh, joy," thought Lucy.

Three Little Words

Amazingly, things went a little more smoothly over the next few days. It helped that Billy's parents took their entire brood with them, including Billy, on a couple of the days when they left in the morning, drawing a thunderous sigh of relief from Lucy and her fellow camp hosts. It also helped that the hosts and some of the campers were beginning to appreciate and understand Billy a little better.

Billy's mistaken Grandma had returned to his end of the campground because her other site had been reserved by someone else. She didn't have any more problems with him and, indeed, seemed to grow fond of his open heart and giant personality. When her stay was over, she left Lucy a note to give the rest of her firewood to his family.

Laura's mother-bird instincts kicked in on Billy's behalf one day when she defended him against some sandbox bullies who were throwing sand and picking on him. You really did not want to ruffle Laura's feathers, especially when it came to protecting a child.

Lucy continued to run interference as best she could with the other campers. One evening she approached an elderly couple sitting under their trailer awning watching the world go by. They were local people and ministered in a small church nearby. They had been married less than a year and were enjoying their first camping trip together.

Lucy recognized the woman as one of the ladies Billy had shown his pet rat to in the pavilion earlier that day. "Loo-oook! It's my pet rat!" He smiled in anticipation of the inevitably funny (to him) reaction.

When Lucy brought up Billy and apologized for the rat incident, the woman softly laughed. "Oh, that didn't bother me. Now don't get me wrong. I'm not fond of rats. But he was just having fun. We've known plenty of children like him before. He meant no harm." The woman's soft face radiated an inner glow.

Lucy and the couple chatted a little longer, and the conversation drifted to tolerance, judgment, and even religion, topics she would normally avoid with strangers, but the flow came naturally, so she went along.

At the conclusion of their chat, the three of them heartily agreed. Only three words were truly needed out of all the holy books in all the history of the whole wide world: God *is* love.

Funny how that God showed up in the darndest of places.

An Angel in a Storm

Lucy tapped away on her computer, keeping an eye on her phone's storm app. The symbol for lightning, high winds, and hail bore down on the little blue dot representing her campground's location.

Outside, complaints about Billy were multiplying like the lightning strikes on her phone screen. Several campers reported that he had asked them for money. One camper said that he would return only if the campground guaranteed that Billy would not be there. Lucy couldn't blame the man for feeling that way. Even though she had gotten used to Billy, she understood that people came to the park to have fun and relax, not to have to deal with him.

Laura was on duty, and Lucy ran over to join her in the campground office. Together, they made sure the campers, especially those in tents, knew of the severe weather alert and where to take shelter if needed.

The storm picked up its wicked pace... wind blowing, lightning flashing, and thunder rumbling. All that energy further electrified the kids playing in the pavilion attached to the office. Billy's family was there—one of their tents had been ruined in a previous storm and they weren't taking any chances—but Billy was the only one you really noticed.

He and Laura's eight-year old daughter, Daisy, raced around the pavilion, dashing in and out of the rain. Billy had his arm out of its sleeve and hidden under his shirt, pretending it had been zapped off by lightning. Daisy laughed wildly.

Billy charged up to the office window and thrust his armless shoulder towards Lucy.

"Sorry, no more band-aids for you, sir," Lucy teased.

Over the past two weeks, Laura had given Billy many band-aids, always in even numbers, because odd numbers were just wrong. Laura understood him very well.

Billy looked at Lucy, disappointment clouding his face.

"I'm just kidding you." Lucy's professional face cracked into a big smile. The storm's energy had affected more than just the kids.

"I know!" he laughed, and he ran off to chase Daisy around the pavilion some more.

A little later, he stuck his head back into the office window and started chattering to Lucy and Laura about all sorts of things. Lucy mostly tuned him out, but at one point he mentioned something about twins.

Lucy jumped at the opening to learn something more about his enigmatic family. "Your brothers are twins?"

Billy looked at her funny. "Nooo, they're not twins!"

"You said something about twins a minute ago..."

"Yeah, my twin sister!"

"You have a twin sister? Which one is she?" Lucy tried to decide if it was the blond or the red-headed girl.

"She's in heaven."

"Oh... I'm sorry."

"She died when we were born. But Mom didn't tell me about it 'til later. I even got to name her."

"What did you name her?"

"Heaven," he replied, with uncharacteristic softness.

At that moment, Lucy glimpsed an angel in Billy.

One

Lucy and Sassy encountered Billy's mother and several of his sisters on their Saturday morning walk. The family was taking a break from their packing to wander around the park before their departure, enjoying the beautiful river and other sights. The mother gave Lucy a polite nod and a simple reply when she wished them safe travels. One of the daughters met her eyes and smiled.

On her way back to her camper, Lucy found Billy dragging blankets and other gear towards the dumpster. The items had been ruined in the series of storms that had passed through the area during their two-week stay.

"Can I have my hug now?" Lucy asked after opening the door to the trash bin for Billy.

"I finally get my hug!" he exclaimed.

A hug can be brief and superficial, like a peck on the cheek. Or it can be a meeting of two hearts.

Billy, being Billy, gave all that he had. Lucy, being Lucy, gave all that she could.

"High five!" Lucy raised her two hands after they let go.

"No! Fist bumps!" he commanded.

Lucy copied Billy's stance. They each held their two clenched fists shoulder height, palm down, and then smashed them together. Hard.

"Again!" he instructed. They smashed again. "See? Odd is bad, even is good. Two fists, two times. That equals four bumps."

"Ah, yes, of course," Lucy smiled. "You take care now... and stay sweet!"

"Always sweet!" Billy grinned, and he took off for the sand box.

"BABYYY!" he yelled, approaching a father sitting on the bench with a baby. When Lucy turned around to look one last time before going in her door, she saw Billy holding the baby and heard the father laugh as Billy went on and on and on about this and that and the other.

Odd isn't always bad, thought Lucy. After all, Billy had given her just one hug. One very special, heartfelt hug.

* * *

LUCY

A Campground Chronicles
Short Story (No. 2)

Anna

"Welcome back, Anna! How have you been?" greeted the tall, gray-haired lady who ruled the terrain behind the campground reception counter. Her businesslike demeanor melted into a genuine smile as Anna Barkley came around to the opening in the counter for a big hug.

"Oh, Miss Lucy, what a day we have had just gettin' here," sighed Anna, a petite, pretty lady with auburn curls. Ron, her rather scruffy, long-haired husband, gave Lucy a quick wave then wandered off to check out the snacks rack.

"Aw, well, I'm glad y'all made it safe and sound. Was the traffic bad on the interstate?" Lucy began gathering the check-in papers.

The Barkleys had reserved three campsites that weekend, one for themselves and the other two for Anna's sisters. It was to be a reunion. They hadn't all been together in one place at the same time since Anna's wedding ten years ago, and she hoped that the get-together would help repair some of the damage that time, carelessness, and neglect had done to their relationships. Now, eight children and six husbands later, the sisters had managed to agree on this one weekend to meet at Sunny Acres, the same campground their parents had taken them to as kids.

Lucy had never met the other sisters, but Anna had filled her in on them during previous visits. The oldest, Diane, was the proud momma of five of those children and possessor of two of the husbands (one at a time, of course, and the second a great improvement over the first). Anna was the middle sister. Lisa, the youngest, proudly bore the label of "problem child." Lisa tore through husbands so fast that she didn't have time to conceive anything warmer than a cold plot to take their money. She was on her third hapless victim.

"No, the traffic wasn't so bad," Anna replied softly, glancing back at Ron, who had moved to the corner of the office/store that stocked fishing equipment. "It's just not easy gettin' outta the house with three boys in tow. If it were, we'd be here a whole lot more than we have been."

Anna and Ron lived in Roanoke, Virginia and came to Sunny Acres at least once a month when the weather was fine. Lucy figured it was their "safe place," where the boys had room to run free, giving the parents a chance to sit, fish, and relax. Ron worked at his father's auto shop and was a very talented mechanic. He seemed to have more rapport with machinery than people, though, from what Lucy had ever observed.

"There now, we're just glad you make it as often as you do," Lucy reassured her, handing Anna three envelopes. "And what a bonus it will be this weekend to have your sisters and their families. I can't wait to meet them. Here you go, hon'. Just put these cards on the posts for sites A-9, 11, and 13. You know where they are, all grouped together on the right side of the first row. And here's the information on park activities this weekend."

"Look, Ron," called Anna, waving one of the flyers. "There's a fishing tournament on Saturday afternoon."

Ron grunted at his wife, nodded at Lucy, and walked out the door, jangling his keys impatiently. Lucy heard the three Barkley boys screaming and laughing when he opened the truck door.

Patting Anna's hand, she said, "You just have yourself a good time, honey. And let me know if you need anything. Anything at all."

"Thanks, Miss Lucy, I will."

Lucy watched Anna climb into the truck. Ron began to pull off before her door was half closed, hauling their 30-foot trailer behind.

Lucy's heart ached.

But she had no time to dwell on that. The front door was busy jingling the arrival of the next guest.

Ed and Trixie

An older couple entered the office hand-in-hand. "Well, I'll be darned if it isn't Ed and Trixie from The Honeymooners," Lucy laughed. Not only were their names really Ed and Trixie, they resembled older versions of the duo by the same name on the 1950's TV show, "The Honeymooners." They were 75-year old newlyweds who had been childhood sweethearts and had rediscovered each other late in life. *Just in time*, Ed liked to say.

"Oh stop, you silly," Trixie chuckled at Lucy. "You aren't the only one giving us that tease. Honestly, this Ed is much better looking than that other old goat."

"Which old goat?" Ed asked, leaning close to his bride of six months. "The TV Ed or that husband of yours you finally tossed out to make room for me?" His eyes twinkled and he patted Trixie's ample rear.

Turning full attention to Lucy, he reached across the counter and took her hand in both of his. "Lucy! This romance stuff ain't for the birds after all. You let me know when you're ready to meet my baby brother, Jack. Oh... Wait a minute... I feel like I'm forgetting something." Ed let a sly smile slip Trixie's way.

Trixie turned her slightly flushed face to Lucy. "Oh, dear. Now, Lucy, don't read too much into it or get tied up in one of your tizzies, but we invited Jack to join us this weekend in the camper..."

Lucy's smile woodened.

It didn't happen often, but an occasional friend or acquaintance would sometimes try to play matchmaker for this odd woman who traveled alone with her dog. They were never successful. Trixie, who had first met Lucy years ago while camping at Sunny Acres with the husband she had before Ed, was perfectly aware of Lucy's feelings on the subject: *If he has his own rig and stays at least six states away from me at all times, then, fine, I'll give it a whirl.*

Lucy put on her professional face and gathered the Gentry's paperwork. "No worries Trixie, Ed. Just sign here, and you know what to do with the rest. There are a lot of great activities planned in the park this weekend to help keep you and any guests you have nicely entertained..." *and out of my hair*, she finished in her head.

During their brief conversation, the door had been very busy. Three more guests had arrived and awaited their turn to check in so they could hurry up and get to their campsites; set up an assortment of motorhomes, tents, trailers, and other such shelters; unload canoes, kayaks, bicycles, satellite dishes, grills, and other such entertainment devices; buy firewood, ice, souvenirs, marshmallows, worms, and... relax. Finally. Relax.

"Fridays are such a challenge," sighed Lucy, peering over Ed and Trixie's shoulders at the growing line. Her scan returned to their friendly, open faces. Lucy softened. "I'll be by to check on you later, my dears. Go. Settle in. And have a lovely time."

Ne-ext

Lucy spent the next five hours greeting, accommodating, and informing a conveyor belt of guests. Many she knew. Some were new to the park. All were welcomed with her competent, well-practiced greeting and smile. All were sent on their way with an overload of information, concise directions, a briefing on park rules and regulations, and a packet of colorful papers.

Anna's two sisters arrived just 30 minutes apart, and they could not have been more different. Diane breezed in with her husband, Dan, and all five of their children. Lucy held her breath until they finally left the office (in one piece, thank heavens), spilling out the door in a pile of laughter and wild energy. They towed a 38-foot toy-hauler behind their truck, complete with bunk beds in which to stuff the kids and a large compartment in the back in which to stuff seven bicycles, three kayaks, and a ton of fishing gear. Lucy could tell they were well-seasoned campers.

Lisa, on the other hand, arrived alone. She pulled up on a motorcycle, expensive-looking backpack strapped to the seat behind her and saddlebags fully loaded. She dismounted and shook her long, bleached blond locks free from her helmet. Lighting a cigarette and drawing a deep puff, she surveyed the campground. If the sour look on her tanned face was any indication, she wasn't impressed. When she finally entered the office, shaking her keys loudly, she drew the rapt attention of several men loitering in the fishing section.

"Welcome to Sunny Acres. How can I help you?" asked Lucy. In her youth, Lucy had owned a motorcycle and traveled solo, too. Her longest trip had been from northern Florida to Key West, where she waitressed for a month until she was fired. She never knew if it was because she was a rotten waitress, or she attracted the wrong kind of clientele—hippy types who nursed one cup of coffee for two hours and wrote poetry to her on napkins. She chose to believe the latter. She suspected the former.

In any case, Lucy looked forward to getting to know this woman's story. Until the woman opened her mouth...

"Uh, yeah, I'm Lisa Hopper and I'm checking in as part of the Barkley group," she spat out, slamming her keys on the counter and giving her long locks another good toss.

She didn't seem very excited to be spending the weekend with her sisters and their broods. When Lucy showed her where to go on the campground map, Lisa asked to change her site to the other side of the campground, but those were all taken. She had to settle for the spot Anna had picked for her, nestled in between her two big sisters and their gigantic families. "Oh, Gawwwd," she whined. "I'm gonna be surrounded by all those kids? What kind of a vacation is tha-at?"

A nice-looking man stood in line behind Lisa, trying not to eavesdrop and looking anywhere but at the little drama on display at the counter. He nimbly stepped aside to avoid getting hit when Lisa swung her suede shoulder-pack on, simultaneously sticking a cigarette between her lips. She lit it before totally out the door, took three deep drags, and tossed it onto the pavement.

Turning her attention to the next guest, Lucy felt the roar of the bike outside resound deeply in her bones.

45

Although they had never met, Lucy recognized Ed's brother, Jack, right away. Trixie had shown her pictures of him from the wedding when she and Ed passed through Sunny Acres on their honeymoon camping excursion last spring. Ed and Jack were very close. When Jack's wife died after a long battle with cancer, he retired from his job in Washington, D.C. and moved to the outskirts of Nashville, Tennessee to be near Ed, the eternal bachelor still residing on the old family farm.

"Hello, you must be Jack," Lucy pre-empted with outstretched hand.

Jack took her hand in a warm, firm grip. "Why, yes. So, you must be Lucy. It's great to finally meet you. Ed and Trixie have told me an awful lot about this area and this campground. They love it here. They think mighty highly of the lady who runs the joint, too." His smile was disarming.

Quickly substituting the campground packet for her hand, Lucy forged ahead. "Yes, it is a lovely campground." She took his packet back and opened it up. "Here is some information on this weekend's activities. The state park has lots of trails, boat and bike rentals, fishing, swimming—although it is a bit chilly for that now—and a few programs that the rangers put on. This one on the reproductive habits of local fauna and flora looks interesting..." Lucy faltered, but only for a moment.

Pulling out a campground map, she grabbed a yellow marker and highlighted his route. "You will find Ed and Trixie in their favorite spot, site A-12, which is on the left side at the end of row A. Most of the roads are one-way, so be careful. Speed limit is 10."

She rattled off a few more mundane details before Jack gently gathered the loose papers, tipped his hat, and stepped aside for the next person in line. "Thank you very much, Miss Lucy. I hope to see you again real soon," he called, waving his packet on the way out.

What an annoying man... Lucy turned her attention back to the conveyor belt.

Sassy VI

Lucy already knew most of the remaining arrivals. After all, she had been employed at Sunny Acres as campground manager for five years and, before that, she camp-hosted there several summers. She traveled much more widely back then, and camp hosting was a great way to control her costs, receiving a free campsite in exchange for helping out in the campground. She had worked at quite a few parks around the country during those first years of travel.

Sunny Acres was always special, though. It was a small campground, part of a state park located on the banks of Lake Wannabellana in east Tennessee's Appalachian Mountains. Lucy had discovered it on one of her trips from the Rio Grande in Texas to the Pocono Mountains in Pennsylvania, two of her other favorite camp-hosting locations. Sunny Acres became a regular stop, convenient for anyone traveling the interstate system that sliced diagonally from the southwestern to northeastern states. Lucy loved the soft, gentle peaks of the Appalachians and their lush, green valleys. While surrounding areas suffered during summer heat waves, this little oasis remained refreshing and relatively cool.

Five years ago, Lucy found it more difficult to finance her traveling lifestyle. Her savings were running low, and camp-hosting was strictly a barter arrangement. So, making the best of her situation, she joined the ranks of snowbird travelers. She traded her motorhome in for a used truck and a small, towed trailer, which she could leave parked in one spot for as long as she wanted. During the six warmest months of the year, May through October, she served as Office Manager at Sunny Acres Campground (a paid position, in addition to the free campsite). From December to March, she managed a small park in east Texas under similar terms.

Each April and November, Lucy wandered a meandering line between her two jobs, carefully towing her trailer behind and exploring as widely as possible along the way. It was a good compromise and helped to make up for her wings being slightly clipped.

Sassy III traveled with Lucy when she switched from camp hosting to paid jobs. Ever since she had lost her original Sassy—her canine companion for the first few years of her travels—Lucy adopted only elderly dogs. She feared she might die and leave her dog behind with no one to love or care for it properly. So, after Sassy passed over the Rainbow Bridge,

Lucy adopted aged dogs, planning to always outlive her best-friend-of-the-moment. Her Sassy.

The only downside was having to mop up her tears each time another Sassy passed on. That, and getting another elderly dog accustomed to a brand-new name. It was like running a hospice for dogs. Dogs named Sassy.

Sassy VI (formerly known as Butternut) snored softly at Lucy's feet when the last guest of the day arrived... on anything *but* a conveyor belt.

Mr. Bojangles

Two minutes before closing time, another motorcycle roared up to the office. Not just any motorcycle. This one defined the word style. Black with silver trim, it sported a jet-black sidecar somewhat shaped like a jet. A stately German Shepherd wearing golden goggles and a red kerchief around its neck occupied the sidecar as if it were a supersonic throne. A tall, black case was strapped in next to the shepherd. Towed behind was a compact, silver trailer about five feet long, four feet wide, and two feet high.

The front door slapped open with a wild jangle. A tall, tanned, tattooed man with a long, silky white ponytail strode up to the counter, looked Lucy straight in the eye, and said, "Darlin', am I ever glad to be here. Would you happen to have a spot for me and my dog for a couple of nights?"

The twinkle in his eyes could open a brand new beer bottle and a sweet old heart in one fell swoop.

Lucy hesitated. She faltered. She swallowed the dry knot that had formed in the pit of her stomach, moved up to her throat, and threatened to pop out of her ears.

God, is this man handsome. I wonder if he's a poet...

Neither of those thoughts actually made it to Lucy's conscious brain, of course. She quickly recovered from her inexplicable discomfort and moved to the computer to check availabilities. Professionalism—her strongest suit—proved an effective defense in all sorts of situations, allowing one to stretch one's arm out as long as possible in order to keep another at a safe distance. This one, she could tell, would require the maximum distance.

"Well," she replied, her eyes glued to the computer screen, "we can accommodate you for one night only. Tomorrow we are full. The sites all have electric and water hookups for $30.00 per night, plus taxes." She glanced up briefly, meeting his dark eyes. "Will that suffice?"

"Sure, that'll suffice! That's all I need," the stranger grinned. "Just somethin' to plug into to keep me and the dog warm when the midnight chill sets in. These old bones aren't what they used to be."

Heavens! Is he planning to use a heater in his tent? That's a fire hazard... This guy is nuts. Lucy tried to remember where she put the number for the local fire department.

"There we are, sweetheart," he said, interrupting Lucy's thoughts. He pulled a loose wad of cash out of his pocket and placed it on the counter.

Lucy peeled the appropriate bills out of the warm stack. "If you would like additional nights, they may become available if there are any cancellations tomorrow. I do need your personal information for our files here. Do you mind giving me your driver's license and I can just copy that?"

Tall, silver, and handsome grinned, handing Lucy his license.

She looked at the card. Bojangles. Robert Bojangles. *Is this guy for real*??? *Great. Mr. Bojangles and his dog have come to dance. He better not be some kind of fancy-pants musician.* Lucy glanced back through the window, confirming what she had feared. That was a guitar case strapped in next to the shepherd.

Lucy's weakness for musicians dated back to her wild and distant youth. In her late teens, she ran off with the bass player in a country-western band and, later, she moved onboard a small, wooden sailboat to live a brief life of romance with a blues guitarist who had captured her heart. She fell in love with her second husband on the dance floor. The first husband, well, he was an aberration.

A portrait of propriety masking her percolating thoughts, Lucy copied the information from the license into her computer then carefully returned the card so that no one's fingers touched anyone else's. "Here you go, Mr. Bojangles."

"Bo, please. It's a lot easier and saves on some of the ribbing. And that's my best bud, Trigger, out there in the sidecar." Bo locked eyes with Lucy, smiled a crooked smile, and slipped his change back deep into his pocket.

"Yes, well, Bo, please keep Trigger leashed and under control at all times," responded Lucy, unlocking Bo's pointed stare.

She continued. "Here is your site on the map. Site A-10. Here is where we are. You turn left here, go to the end and turn right. Yours will be the second-to-last spot on the left. There are loads of children in the campground this weekend, so please drive carefully. This is your tag for the post and some information about park activities for the weekend." She slapped the packet down on the counter more forcefully than she had intended. "Please let us know if you need anything more."

"That I will, darlin'. Thank you very kindly." With a deep nod, a turn, and a skip, Bo jangled out the door.

Lucy watched through the front window as he fired up his bike and purred around the corner. For the second time that day, her heart ached.

She popped a baby aspirin, locked the front door, and pulled the shades.

EZ-Come, EZ-Go

In more ways and more places than she could count, Lucy was all tuckered out. It had been an unusually busy Friday and extra stress had been added because the camp host, Joe, had taken the afternoon off. Lucy and Joe worked great together, with Joe concentrating on the condition of the campground and on campers' needs after check-in. He had to take his wife, Elle Mae, to the doctor that afternoon, though, and had not returned by 7:00 when the office closed. Lucy prepared to do evening rounds in his place.

Nudging her worries on Joe and Elle Mae's behalf to the side, Lucy climbed into the EZ-Go work cart. Sassy lumbered into her travel bed on the passenger floor. Slightly bigger and more powerful than a golf cart, the EZ-Go was the envy of all the children in the campground. Kids on bicycles loved to race it from behind. More than once, she almost slaughtered a young lad by abruptly applying her brakes, unaware that the boy had been riding right on her tail.

List in hand, Lucy and Sassy puttered through the campground, checking all the sites, ensuring that people were settling in all right, and fielding questions here and there. She gave a quick wave to Ed, Trixie, and Jack. The brothers were busy building their fire. Trixie bustled between the camper and the picnic table.

Glancing at their neighbor's site, she did a double take. Bo had transformed his little trailer into an amazing contraption: a tent straight out of *Dances With Wolves* meets *Arabian Nights* meets *Mad Max*.

The central part of the floor was the trailer bottom, stabilized with an adjustable leg on each corner. Each of the four trailer walls were folded down, creating more floor space, supported from beneath by more stabilizer legs. Fiberglass walls rose two feet straight up from each edge, and then heavy canvas continued the rise, angling to meet at a peak six or seven feet from the floor of the trailer. Large, screened windows with canvas rain flaps were set into each wall and, although she couldn't see it directly, there must have been an access door of some sort in the rear.

"Ahhhh!!!" screamed a little boy. Lucy swerved just in time to miss him as he and his bike took a spill in front of her.

She mashed the brakes and jumped out of her cart. "Are you OK, honey?"

"Yeah, I'm fine," he bravely proclaimed, picking up his bike and peeling off in the other direction.

Well, that's the first time I almost ran one over. Damn that crazy old man and his eyesore of a tent!

"Jason! Is that you?" Anna came running from her campsite on the other side of the lane.

"Oh, Anna, I'm so sorry," said Lucy. "I'm pretty sure he's fine. I didn't hit him; he just fell off his bike. He got right back on and took off again. That way."

"Don't worry, Miss Lucy. That kid's as tough as they come. He shouldn't be ridin' anymore, though. It's too dark out."

"I'll send him back home when I run across him... um, when I see him again, dear," Lucy reassured Anna. She climbed back into the EZ-Go and checked on Sassy who, fortunately, had been curled up in her travel bed when the near-collision had occurred. Although startled, she was none the worse for wear.

Before Lucy could resume her circuit, Trixie's voice called out from behind.

"Lucy, honey, come by for a spell after you make your rounds. We'll be having dinner in 30 minutes or so and would love for you to join us. You work so hard. You deserve a nice break. Sassy, you're invited too!"

Sassy thumped her tail, looked hopefully at Lucy, and drooled.

Turning to face her friend, the stress of Lucy's day melted into gratitude for the simple things in life: friendship, generosity, fresh air, and good food. Her stomach growled in agreement.

"Sure, Trixie. And thanks. We'll be back in a bit." She drove off to complete her rounds, keeping an eye out for Jason and his bicycle.

Firelight, Moonlight

Firelight is magic
Moonlight, hypnotic
Prepare yourself
For they can weave a spell
To take your heart places you do not intend
Even if you are prepared...
Beware...
For firelight is tricky
Moonlight, fickle
Some of their abodes can be very, very dark
Others, bright, yes...
But shifting...
Beware those shadows dancing

Lucy and Sassy returned half an hour later with a bottle of wine. Ed and Trixie's fire blazed golden and red. Ed flipped burgers on the grill over the flames. Jack stood nearby, beer in one hand, platter filled with open buns in the other. He waved at Lucy with his beer.

Trixie was setting all the fixin's on a small folding table: fried tomatoes, onions, and mushrooms; lettuce, pickles, and slices of cheese; deviled eggs, potato salad, and baked beans. A red-and-white checkered tablecloth dressed up the old picnic table, pairs of colorful cups and plates carefully set on each side. In the center, three kinds of pie circled around a beautiful old, oil-filled lantern. It was a delectable picture of wild domesticity.

"Lucy, Sassy, welcome! Come on over here, girl." Trixie bent down to accept Sassy's wet kiss right on the lips. She reached into her apron pocket and slipped her a couple of dog treats while Lucy secured her leash to a small tree nearby.

"Oh, my, what a long day that was," Lucy sighed, sinking into Trixie's hug. "Thanks for the invite, Trixie... Sorry I was a bit of a pill back there when you checked in."

"Think nothing of it, sweetie. You know we love you, and that's all that matters." Trixie kissed Lucy lightly on the cheek.

"Save some of that sugar for the chef!" roared Ed. He cleared a spot on the side table for Jack's platter of burgers. "Come and get it before this table collapses, eh?"

Plates filled, toasts given, and doggy fed (Sassy got two burgers all to herself), the group set into their meal.

"There's nothing like eating home-cooked goodness under the starlight," sighed Trixie.

"Nope, nothing like it, my sweet," responded Ed between bites, "except for some home-spun badness under the sheets later!"

"Oh, Ed. Control yourself, you old dog!" Trixie's elbow found its mark and Ed nearly dropped the piece of pie he had been carefully guiding to his plate.

"Another toast," said Jack, raising his cup. His companions followed suit.

"To love, at any age, any stage... It's all the rage, I hear..." He cracked a smile and looked to Lucy for help.

She jumped right in: "So quell that fear and grab a beer..."

Trixie quickly finished: "Love me... 'til the last page, my dear!"

After eating more than their fill, everyone pitched in to clean things up, then gathered close around the campfire. They laughed some more, ate some more, and shared more stories.

Ed told of his and Jack's youth, growing up on their family's tobacco farm. It was hard work and, although they were five years apart, the boys stuck close together. Their mom worked doubly hard, teaching school, then returning home to all the tasks of a farmer's wife. She made sure the brothers didn't neglect their schoolwork, and both boys were the first of the Gentry clan to attend college.

Ed teased Jack about his choice to move to the big city after graduation.

Jack teased Ed about waiting 75 years to get married.

"I can't help it that my sleeping beauty was lost in the woods for so long." Ed reached over and took Trixie's hand. She raised it to her lips and lightly kissed his fingers.

Over the years of their friendship, Lucy had learned much of Trixie's story—the good, the bad, and the ugly. Ed's tales painted another piece of the portrait. Lucy was thrilled for Trixie, picturing her good friend with her true love, together forever, on the old family farm. Sure, the picture was overly romanticized, but how could you help it on a night like this... *Just look at that moon...*

Lucy glanced across the lane. Anna and Diane and their families were having a fine time, too. Jason, who seemed to have taken no permanent damage from the run-in with Lucy's EZ-Go, chased a small shaggy dog, trying alternately to tempt it with bits of food and to tie a rope around its neck. The other children flew all over the place, like pixies dodging between firelight and shadow, enjoying the night as only a fearless innocent can.

She was surprised to see that Bo was part of the group, entertaining the adults around the campfire with his guitar and a soft song. Anna and Diane were lost in the embrace of their husbands, slow-dancing under the watchful moon.

Lisa hovered close to Bo, trying to sing harmony. Even from a distance, it sounded slightly off key. But the firelight took no notice. It traced a delicate dance on her long blond hair, and the song rose to the stars on children's laughter and wisps of hope.

Jack

Lucy and Sassy woke early the next morning. Lucy prepared a quick breakfast, put on her walking shoes and a broad-brimmed hat, and strapped Sassy into her harness.

"Okay, girl, time for the best part of the day." She grabbed a plastic bag and her trash picker-upper and opened the door. On good days, Sassy could walk a couple of miles. This looked to be an excellent day.

Her trailer was parked in the front part of the campground, not too far from the entrance and the office. Walking towards the trailhead in the back corner, Lucy relished the sleepy peace that curled in and around each campsite. A few smoky tendrils hovered above an occasional smoldering campfire. Not even a dog barked.

Ten minutes later, they cleared the trees and arrived at the path that embraced the lake. With no wind, the water served as mirror to the drifting fog, the boundary between reflection and reality impossible to discern. The mountains across the lake reflected as dark shadows, their early autumn colors unable to penetrate the thick wisps of mist rising from the glassy surface below.

"No matter how many mornings we come here, girl, it's always a fresh sight." Sassy sniffed the base of a tree and lifted her leg to pee. She didn't get much height on it, despite her best efforts.

"Come on, you old goose," Lucy laughed, "let's get a good walk in while we can." She worked from noon until 6:00 today—not as bad as a Friday, but still a long stretch with no break—and she wanted to make the most of the morning with her best friend.

Sassy leading the way, they made it to the swimming beach about a mile up the trail before Lucy turned them around. "Good walkin' there, girl, but remember, we've gotta make it back."

"Hi ho! Good morning!" sounded a familiar voice. Jack, walking stick in one hand, camera in the other, approached from further up the trail. As he neared, Lucy noticed what beautiful, piercing blue eyes he had. She was surprised she hadn't noticed them when he checked in.

"I can't get over what a gorgeous place this is," Jack sighed, reaching Lucy and turning to look at the lake. "I think I've taken more pictures this morning than I have in the past year. And how are you and Miss Sassy this fine day?" He turned and smiled at her warmly.

"Couldn't be better," Lucy said, meaning every word, but fighting the urge to back up three steps. "I think this little lake is one of nature's finest works, and this is the season it shows its prettiest face. We're lucky the park service has all the property surrounding it, so no one has been able to muck it up... although, they do keep on trying!" She waved her bag filled with bits of trash collected on her walk.

Jack shook his head. "Well, you just can't cure stupid."

"Or fix dumb," she laughed.

"Or dictate respect," he added.

"Or solve sick-in-the-head," she countered.

"Or... or..."

"Or stand here all morning when there's work to be done," Lucy finished with a flourish of her trash picker-upper, nearly smacking Jack in the head.

"Work? Today? Whenever do you get a day off, dear woman?" Jack placed his hand gently on her weapon arm.

Lucy backed up two steps.

"Hey, it's Saturday. Busy, busy day in a campground. Not so many checking in, but there's ice and wood and worms to sell and questions to answer and loads of people to chat with. Mine is a very important job. Quite a step up from when I used to camp host and

61

clean bathrooms, fire rings, and grills. Now I can do all that, and more!" she laughed. "In fact, we were just going to head back when you showed up."

"Okay, boss. I'm smart enough not to question credentials. Will it be all right if I join you on the return walk?"

"Sure, as long as you don't mind a tired old dog's pace."

"Sounds about my speed," he smiled.

The trio leisurely returned to the campground. Jack took more photos, including some of Sassy. Lucy added to her trash bag. And Sassy left her two scents on all the best spots along the trail.

They talked a little about the lake, photography, dogs, best friends, and brothers. During wordless spells, they enjoyed an easy silence. By the time Jack left Lucy at her trailer, the sun had risen to mid-morning height, and the campground was awake and abuzz with activity.

In fact, it wasn't too far into Lucy's second cup of coffee when she heard gunshots.

Wanna Banana

Lucy grabbed her phone and her keys and ran out the door. For a moment, she was totally disoriented. She didn't see the EZ-Go in the spot she had parked it last night. *Oh my God, did someone steal that old thing?* Then it occurred to her that Joe must have returned and collected it when she was out for her walk so that he could do his morning camp host rounds.

She half-ran, half-walked towards the office, trying to determine the direction the shots had come from and watching for signs that would help her know where to go. As she neared the office, she heard another shot and yelling from the far corner of the campground—the direction of Ed and Trixie's site.

Now she ran. Somehow, she found the presence of mind to dial 911. When the operator answered, she had to slow to a walk in order to talk. Even then, she could barely get her words out while gulping for air. *Boy, regular walks may be good for the heart, but they don't do much for the lungs when the going gets really rough*, her thoughts raged.

"Emergency operator. What is your emergency?"

"I don't know. I'm not sure yet. Gunshots. I'm on my way there now," she huffed.

"Where are you located and what is the nature of your emergency?"

"Sunny Acres Campground. On Lake Wannabellana. I don't know yet... I'm walking as fast as I can," she puffed.

"Lake Wanna Banana?"

"Lake Wannabellana!!!" she screamed.

"What is the nature of your emergency?"

"Gunshots. Sunny Acres Campground. Just get here!!!" Lucy threw the phone to the ground and tried to pick up speed. She rounded the corner and found Ed and Trixie outside their trailer watching the spectacle unfold one campsite over. Ed stood protectively in front of Trixie, who peeked out from his side.

Jack stood in the driveway of Bo's site. Joe, sitting in the EZ-Go, was next to him. They spoke softly to one another. Just in front of them, a man brandishing a handgun paced back and forth before Bo's fancy-tent.

"Come on out of there, Lisa," he yelled, shooting another round into the air.

Silence. Even the birds had stopped their song.

The silence was finally broken by Jack.

"Sir, please put the gun down. I know you don't want to hurt any innocents. This campground is filled with women and children, and you wouldn't want to see a bullet fall from the sky and hurt someone, now, would you?"

The man slowly turned towards Jack. He looked amazed that anyone else was present, let alone a growing crowd of nervous onlookers.

Jack added, more softly this time, "Really, sir, let me give you a hand. Come. Sit down. Talk to me." He walked over to Bo's picnic table and took a seat on the bench. Hands raised, he motioned the gunman over.

Lucy couldn't tell if it was her heart that jumped or if she was feeling the reverberating shock from Ed and Trixie's hearts.

The crowd emitted a collective gasp as the gunman slowly walked to the table and sat down opposite Jack. He placed the gun between them.

Then he laid his head down, covered it with his arms, and silently wept.

Owen

Lucy, her breath coming in a painful wheeze now rather than ragged gulps, simply walked over and sat on the other side of the broken man. She draped her arm around his back and gently rested her head on his shoulder.

And said nothing.

While the man's attention was diverted by this odd, wheezing old woman who came out of nowhere to offer him comfort, Jack slid the gun down onto the bench beside him. He continued to speak softly. The man's quiet sobs pierced Lucy's racing heart like a twisting knife.

It seemed an eternity passed. The growing crowd, silenced by the unfolding drama, cushioned the little spectacle from the outside world.

Finally, a smoky voice drifted out from the depths of the fancy-tent.

"Owen, honey, I'm really sorry..."

Owen. What a nice name for such a tragic fellow, Lucy thought. She softly rubbed Owen's shoulder.

Owen slowly lifted his head. He looked around for his gun. He didn't seem to mind that it was no longer there. He stood up, left Lucy and Jack, and shuffled a few steps in the direction of his wife's voice.

"Come on out of there, Lisa. The least you can do is talk to me face-to-face."

Minutes impersonating hours strolled by.

"Why'd you have to go and take my bike?" he finally continued. "You could've wrecked it..."

Owen began to sway, slowly, side-to-side.

No one breathed.

"Leeesaaaaaahhh...," he screamed.

Sirens broke through from a distance, quickly closing in with their frantic tempo and ragged harmony.

Joe, who had carefully approached Jack and Lucy when Owen got up, grabbed the gun from beside Jack's thigh. He climbed back into the EZ-Go and high-tailed it out of there to meet the police.

When the police arrived and worked through the crowd of gawking, chattering campers, they arrested-without-incident Owen Emory Hopper, husband of Lisa Rebecca Hopper, father of none.

It wasn't hard. Owen was on his knees, openly sobbing... like a gaping wound, with no healing, no recourse in sight but to survive the long march of time. A wheezing woman knelt beside him, arm around his shoulders, shielding him from the merciless crowd.

MPCADC

Sharing a life-or-death, operatic-worthy experience should really bond one soul to another's. Maybe not forever, but at least for a few days, you would think.

Under ordinary circumstances it might, or with ordinary people. But not if one of those souls belonged to the Mistress of Professionally Cold Analytic Defense Capabilities. Goodness, that could be an actual job title in some big government agency.

Owen was taken away to county lock-up. Bo stood outside his tent door speaking to the officers with Lisa, who remained inside the tent. When Lisa finally emerged, she kissed Bo deeply in front of the murmuring crowd then sauntered back to her campsite across the lane. She mounted Owen's motorcycle and roared off after the Sherriff's parade, her long blond locks flicking a proverbial finger at the trailing onlookers. A couple of officers stayed behind to take more statements.

My, that girl sure knows how to make an exit, thought Lucy.

Oddly, Trigger was nowhere to be seen or heard.

As the crowd finally began to disperse, Bo returned to his fancy-tent without acknowledging anything was out of the ordinary. His hair, free from its ponytail, shone as slightly yellowed silver in the mid-day sun. His tattoos, free from a shirt, stood out in slightly sagging, crinkled glory.

All in a day's work, I suppose, Lucy snorted to herself, fighting angry, protesting leg muscles while trying to rise from the bench where she had been talking to Trixie.

Jack reached to help her up. She brushed him off like a fly on a hamburger.

"That's all right. No need," she bristled. "I'll be up at the office if anyone needs me," she announced to no one in particular.

Thankfully, Joe had returned with the EZ-Go and gave her a ride.

Joe and Elle Mae

"How did things go yesterday?" Lucy asked Joe, unlocking the office. They had retrieved Sassy on the way, along with Lucy's phone, or what was left of it. It had been smashed by all the traffic surrounding the incident.

"Is Elle Mae all right?" Lucy was intent upon discussing anything other than what they had both just witnessed. She never was one for gossip. Even less so when it concerned an obviously painful, highly personal subject.

"Yup, she's gonna be fine," Joe replied in his indeterminable accent. "Thanks for filling in for me last night. I hope it wasn't too much trouble. The doctor was running late and then we had a flat tire on the way back. I'd be complaining about our bad luck if it weren't for what we saw out here today. Lord, it's things like that that make me appreciate my Elle Mae more than ever. I sure hope she feels the same," he chuckled.

"I know that she does," reassured Lucy, firing up the computer. "You two were a match made in heaven before the earth was ever born. I've never seen two people more suited to one another and more loving. It's all the more amazing as you've been together so long. Most people would have killed each other by now."

Joe's eyes sparkled. "Yeah, we were high school sweethearts. Known each other fifty-some years now. Heck, we've got a big wedding anniversary coming up."

"Oh yeah? When? Will it be your fiftieth?"

"Yup, a week from Sunday, if I remember rightly."

Lucy scribbled a small note so that precious piece of information would not be lost in the clutter of every-day living.

"I like to think that Ed and Trixie would be just like you and Elle Mae if they hadn't lost all those years before finding each other again. In fact, if y'all were paintings, you and Elle Mae would be done in oil. Ed and Trixie... Ed and Trixie would be a watercolor," she concluded with a firm nod of her head.

Joe shook his head and softly laughed. "Lucy, sometimes I think you think waaay too much." He grabbed a bag of chips, put his money on the counter, and waved goodbye, leaving the office to do his rounds.

Lucy opened the blinds and reflected on the vagaries of love. The mid-day glare was too intense. She quickly folded them closed, shutting out the sun.

Daylight

As far as Saturdays went, this one went down in Sunny Acres' history as the most exciting, exhausting, terror-and-fun-filled Saturday in at least a decade.

Mr. Bojangles and his illicit tryst with Lisa Hopper was the talk of the campground. And, whether she liked it or not, much of that talk centered in the environs of Lucy's camp store/office.

She could not escape the chatter:

"Ooooo, did you see his tattoos?"

"Yeah, that snake with the triple fang means he killed somebody!"

"I believe that. Did you hear his dog is trained to kill on command?"

Lucy quickly interjected. "That dog is deaf and blind and slept through the entire fiasco." She had gathered that tidbit from Trixie, who had dropped in to check on her a bit ago. No need to drag the poor dog into this ugly, man-made mess.

Buzz kill.

That's all right, figured Lucy. *Mission accomplished. Even if only temporarily.*

Before the clamor resumed a full roar, Anna, Ron, and Jason entered the office. Jason led a small, shaggy gray dog on a loosely tied rope. His parents held hands. Coming as close as she could to Lucy, Anna whispered over the counter, "Oh, Miss Lucy, please forgive us for Lisa's wild behavior. Diane and I are just so ashamed." Ron wrapped his arm protectively around Anna's waist.

Lucy took Anna's hands in hers and whispered back. "Sweetheart, don't you give it a second thought. It was nobody's fault but those two lunatics... and nobody's business but their *own*," she loudly added, glaring pointedly at the crowd that was edging closer to the counter.

"Aw, thanks Lucy. You're a gem." Anna squeezed then released Lucy's hands. "Lisa ain't comin' back tonight, by the way. She said to just let Jason here and the other kids have her tent and camping gear. Jason slept in it already last night with this furry little monster he caught. They were supposed to be with Aunt Lisa, but, well..."

Jason could wait no longer and interrupted. "Miss Lucy, look! Look at this!" Proudly holding up his end of the rope, Jason firmly directed his companion to sit. The shaggy lump promptly sat, his long tail raising an army of dust bunnies on the floor behind. "See how smart he is? Ma, Pa, come on, let me keep him, pleeeaaase?" Jason's puppy dog eyes rivaled those of the real puppy dog's eyes.

"Sorry, baby, but we gotta see if he belongs to someone. Maybe he's just lost. Anyhow, we ain't got room for another dog, especially not a young pup like that."

Turning back to Lucy, Anna said, "We're gonna run him up to the vet in town real quick and see if he's got one of them chips in him. If he don't, do you mind if we bring him back to see if one of the other campers here might want him? I don't have the heart to turn him over to the shelter. You know what they do there," she added with a whisper.

Lucy reluctantly agreed, hoping that the little furball indeed had a chip and was simply lost. She wished them luck and gave Jason a bag of pretzels to cheer him up. "Don't you feel bad, now, sweetie. You're doing the right thing," she called after them as they walked out the door. Her encouraging comment could have been meant for any one of the three.

Midafternoon, much to the delight of the milling, murmuring crowd, Mr. Bojangles himself appeared in the office.

Lucy was prepared, pre-empting him before he reached the counter. "You do know that check-out was at 1:00, sir. Your site has been rented for the night, so you need to leave as soon as possible."

"No worries, sweetheart. I've already packed up my gear and Trigger and I are ready to roll, if need be. This is an awfully nice campground you have here, though," he commented, looking around and nodding at some of the gawkers. "If any of those cancellations you mentioned yesterday came through, I sure would like to have a site for another night."

Lucy met his eyes. Not comfortable with conflict, it wasn't easy.

"Sir, given the events of last night and the trouble this morning, I would think that you would be happy to be on your way."

"Ma'am, I am quite happy any which way. But, if you don't mind, I'd like to stay here for another night. I wasn't charged with any crime, so that misunderstanding this morning shouldn't be a problem. As for the 'events of last night,' I didn't notice anything illegal or rowdy. Am I wrong?"

"Mr. Bojangles," Lucy spoke with a measured, firm voice. "Whether by intention or not, that 'misunderstanding this morning' was scandal on the one hand and tragedy on the other.   This is a peaceful, family campground.   Please understand, we have certain standards to upkeep. We have children to protect."

"Yes, ma'am, I understand. I promise to be on my best behavior." Leaning one elbow on the counter, he continued more quietly. "Furthermore, I offer my deepest apologies for any and all discomfort my actions may have caused to those of innocent or delicate constitution..."

Lucy stood her ground and said nothing.

More softly yet: "...but, please, is there a site available for just one more night? Trigger isn't feeling up to the road today."

Lucy looked out the window. Trigger was curled up in the sidecar, napping under a warm blanket. His head rested awkwardly against the guitar case. His golden goggles sat lopsidedly on his face.

Lucy's arched brow relaxed, and she shifted her attention to her computer screen.

"Site F-11 is free due to a cancellation. Here it is on the map. That will be $31.50 including tax, please."

Bo quickly pulled the wad of cash out of his pocket and placed it on the counter.

Lucy waited.

He cracked a small smile and counted the money out, handing it to Lucy.

She deposited it into the register drawer and gave him his new site tag, along with a business card for the local vet.

"Thank you kindly, ma'am."

"You are welcome, sir." She paused. She sighed... "And good luck with Trigger."

All hell broke loose once Bo walked out the door:

"Ooooo, Miss Lucy! What're we gonna do now?"

"Fire up the entertainment, that's what!"

"What entertainment, you idiot! That man's gonna burn in hell sooner than I can smack you with this purse..."

"Quiet!" Lucy shouted. "No violence, please. Stop all this gossip. Go fishing, hiking... Take a cold swim. Take a hot nap. I don't care. But, unless you plan to buy something in the next three minutes, kindly leave this place. Now!"

Fifteen out of twenty people left.

The remaining five milled around, fingering the goods, muttering to one another about mean old Miss Lucy. They finally left, too, belatedly joining the crowd gathering around F-11 to participate in the most popular Saturday activity ever recorded in the annals of Sunny Acres Campground: Watch Mr. Bojangles reconstruct his fancy-tent.

Thankfully, there was to be no more gunfire.

Brown Paper Bag

Five minutes before closing, Trixie came in the front door with a gentle jingle and a brown paper bag. "Okay, Missy, close it up. No one is behind me and your workday has gone on long enough." She flipped the "Open" sign to

"Closed," slid the deadbolt on the door and began pulling down shades.

Knowing better than to question Trixie on a mission, Lucy filled Sassy's bowl with kibbles and grabbed a couple of wine glasses from the top shelf of her cleaning cabinet. With a deep sigh, she sank into one of the easy chairs that sat in the corner of the room where the book exchange shelves stood. Trixie already occupied the other chair and was concentrating on uncorking a bottle of merlot. It was not an unfamiliar routine for the two friends.

Trixie raised her glass: "To Mr. Fancy-pants."

"I thought it was Fancy-tent," Lucy laughed, "but I like yours better."

The friends giggled, clinked glasses, and drank deeply.

"Oh, before I forget..." Trixie pulled a box of saltines and a package of cheese out of the bag. "There. Now we can have two glasses!"

Lucy laughed. The stress of the day began to loosen its grip. "Whoever said that laughter is the best medicine deserves a Nobel Peace Prize."

"Yeah," responded Trixie. "That guy and the one who invented wine."

"In moderation, of course," toasted Lucy to the air.

"Or not," returned Trixie and her glass.

After a few minutes of relaxed conversation, Trixie broached a subject that had been on her mind for some time.

"Lucy, honey, I really don't want to pry, but I just don't understand why you're so... so *hard* when it comes to men."

That gave Lucy pause. It wasn't something she talked about very often, even with a close friend. After giving it some thought, she carefully replied. "I don't think of it as hard. I think of it as strong. I guess I'm just one of those people who likes to be in control.

"When I really think about it, I believe I was the one who left in most of the relationships I've had. Well, heck, it was usually for a darned good reason. The guy cheated on me or was nasty somehow. Or both. I've never been the type to sit still and take that kind of behavior for long. That's not being hard. It's being strong. And smart. At least, that's the way I see it."

Lucy looked to Trixie for agreement. "You'll get no argument from me on that," accommodated Trixie. "I sat around way too long with Mr. Number Two," as she liked to call her second husband.

The friends laughed softly.

Encouraged, Lucy continued. "In fact, the very first boy that I had a crush on... back when I was 12 or 13 years old... He was a year or two older than me. We lived on a dead-end street surrounded by a farmer's fields and woods. It was our love of nature that bonded us. I wandered those woods quite a bit by myself, but sometimes we would walk them together.

"Well, he eventually got in with a fast crowd. A couple of girls that lived across the street from him were drinkers. They'd steal stuff from their parents' liquor cabinet and party it up.

"One day I was out walking the fields and this boy, his younger brother, and those two girls followed me out. They caught up to me and he tackled me to the ground.

"He climbed on top of me, and he started to choke me.

"He wanted me to say out loud that I didn't like him. I guess to please the girls he was with.

"That's all I had to do to get him to stop choking me.

"Say that I didn't like him.

"I wouldn't say it.

"Not so much because I particularly liked him at that moment. It was more because I didn't want him to win. He could have killed me then and there, but as long as I didn't say what he wanted me to say, I would win.

"His brother finally pulled him off of me, and they all left.

"When I got home, I cleaned myself up and didn't say anything to anybody about what had happened. Thankfully, turtleneck shirts were in style and the weather was chilly, so I wore a lot of those until the bruises faded."

Trixie softly interrupted. "You didn't tell your Mom? Your Dad?"

"No. Momma was in the middle of her first battle with cancer. Daddy was trying to take care of her, the household, and his business, all at the same time. I didn't want to add to all of that.

"No. Instead I got strong. Momma had an old, incredibly heavy Royal typewriter. I'd lie on my back on the floor every day and lift that thing like it was a set of barbells. I got so strong that I almost beat my Dad at arm wrestling.

"Better yet, I arm-wrestled that boy later, and I beat him.

"For a second time."

Trixie shook her head slowly. She leaned over and took Lucy's hand in both of hers. "Yeah, honey. You're right. You're not hard. You're about as soft as they come. And as strong. You just do what you've gotta do, because that's you. And I love you. That's why I want to see you happy.

"Go ahead and blame my newly-wedded bliss, but you have to admit that I've been around the block a few times myself. And some of those blocks were mighty hard runs, especially that last one. Still, the love and companionship of a mate—a good, solid man like my Ed or, dare I say it, like Jack—can be such a blessing. It can be worth the risk.

"I know Ed and I have limited time together. And I know it's gonna be real hard when one of us gets torn up by illness and leaves the other one behind. But I have no doubt, none whatsoever, that it'll be worth it to have enjoyed every minute of each other's company for whatever time we have left. What, in heaven's name, could be more precious than that?"

The two friends sat together in silence for a few minutes. Then Lucy rose, retrieved a box of tissues from the desk, and vigorously blew her nose. She passed the box to Trixie, nudged Sassy awake, and gathered her keys and belongings.

Trixie put the empty bottle and unopened cheese and crackers back into the brown paper bag.

Locking the door on the way out, the friends walked arm-in-arm. Sassy, following her nose, led the way. They arrived at Trixie's campsite, where Ed and Jack were flipping burgers over a glowing fire.

A shaggy gray mutt was sitting at Jack's feet.

Sunday Morning

Lucy adored Sundays. It was the first of her two days off. The campground typically emptied, or nearly so, becoming an entirely different place from its Friday through Saturday face. Birdsong and the flitter of leaves falling from trees subdued the echo of wild children taking their final spin on bikes and scooters.

It was a little saddening, though, to see the serious faces of the adults concentrating on packing everything up while, in the back of their minds, they faced a return to their Monday through Friday grind. Packing up on a damp morning or, worse, after a rainy night was hardest on the tent campers. Lucy felt reassured that at least they knew where to return for respite and rejuvenation, whether to

Sunny Acres or—in Bo's case, hopefully—to a perfectly nice park somewhere else.

Joe and Elle Mae took their time on Sunday, the busiest day of their week, working together to clean the vacated sites and fire rings. Sometimes it took them two days to finish them all. But there was no rush. Even in the summer months, weekdays were gratefully slow and easy.

Ed, Trixie, and Jack had decided to stay another couple of days. They planned to explore the local area with Lucy, who knew all of the most beautiful spots 50 miles in any direction.

Lucy was looking forward most, though, to the start of *this* day: a Sunday morning walk along the lake with Jack and the dogs.

As if on cue, at 8:00 sharp, Jack tapped on Lucy's door.

"Boy, are *you* prompt," she smiled broadly, opening the door to sunshine and a fresh breeze.

Furball sat patiently at Jack's side, fitted with a proper collar and a regulation-length leash. His wild coat had been thoroughly washed and brushed. The little guy almost looked handsome. Sassy stuck her big nose out the door, gave a huge sneeze, then jumped outside and covered the pup in kisses. Lucy followed, laughing, leash in hand.

"Yeah, I guess all those years working in a large government office, 9 to 5, had a lasting effect," Jack commented.

"Don't tell me. FBI?" She raised one eyebrow.

"How did you guess?"

"Hostage negotiator, right?"

"What are *you*? CIA?

"Actually, yeah, I spent a few years there." Lucy winked and pulled ahead by a step or two.

Unsure if she was kidding or serious, Jack decided to leave the rest of *that* conversation for another day.

"Speaking of jobs, former and current, where is your weapon today?"

"It's my day off, thank you very much," Lucy called back. "No trash to pick up today. All trash, ugliness, and cray-cray is invisible to my eyes." She waved her free arm leisurely at the mountains, the lake, and the sky.

Letting the boys catch up, Lucy reached down to scratch Furball behind his ears. Sassy lifted her leg for the umpteenth time.

"So," she asked, "have you decided what you're going to call this little guy? Furball is a bit insulting, and a name is an important matter."

"Mmm, yes, I suppose the mom of Sassy VI knows all about that sort of thing," Jack teased.

"Well, you may have me there," Lucy admitted. "It's not from lack of imagination, mind you. I think I just sort of got stuck... Stop changing the subject. What are you going to name him? Do you know?"

"Let's just say that I am happy that it's your day off and that you are weaponless..."

Lucy's eyes widened. "No... You wouldn't... You didn't..."

"Come along *Bo*," Jack called to the pup, who was trailing behind, sniffing Sassy's handiwork with intense interest. "We have a long walk ahead of us, and we don't want to keep the ladies waiting."

* * *

SASSY

A Campground Chronicles
Short Story (No. 3)

Sassy

Sassy stared hard at Lucy. A string of saliva dripped from the corner of her graying snout, dribbled through a span of anticipatory air, and landed on her left front paw. She paid no mind to the warm wetness trickling through her toes, forming a widening pond beneath. More important things were on her mind.

Mmmm... Mom put something special in the eggs today... Bacon! Ya, that's it, bacon! Drop it, Mom, please, drop it drop it drop it drop it... Just one piece, that's all I ask...

"Here we go, girl." Lucy slid the bacon and cheese omelette onto her plate. She mixed some cold water and kibble into the egg mixture still in the pan, then turned to Sassy. "Have at it, Miss Prewash."

Sassy went airborne, the slippery puddle only costing an inch or so in altitude. She landed at the same time as the pan and immediately set to work. For a "mature" dog, she was very athletic.

"Gotta eat fast, baby. That office won't open itself."

After Lucy finished her eggs—Sassy beat her by a mile—she began gathering their things for the day: Her cap with the Sherwood Forest Campground logo on the front and an opening for her long silver ponytail to pop out the back. A score of keys hanging on a ring clipped to her belt loop. Sassy loved the jingle they made. She felt it announced her mom as someone important: Campground Boss. (Sassy was very conscious of the social hierarchy.) Two containers with snack and lunch items for each of them, to be stored in the office refrigerator. And, best of all, leash and fanny pack containing enough poop bags and cookies to cover the day's walks and treats.

Sherwood Forest was their winter campground in east Texas, so there was no need for the b'air horn that Lucy attached to her belt loop when they worked their summer job in Tennessee. Sassy had never seen a bear, but she had heard plenty of campers share their stories. She wondered if they were like horses. Horses were huge, but they didn't scare her one bit. She was certain she could handle a bear, if need be. *Lemme at 'im!*

Sassy would be needing every ounce of that courage soon enough. Fortunately, she—and her Mom—would not be alone. No. Never alone.

Sherwood Forest

"Hello. Welcome to Sherwood Forest Campground. How can I help you?"

Sassy admired Lucy's way with people when they were at work. Always so polite and helpful. More efficient than friendly, but Sassy rounded out the team in that department. Putting on her sweetest face, Sassy rose from her bed and poked her nose around the corner of the counter. Her tail-wag wiggled its way up her spine, tickled the back of her neck, and escaped from her snout with a wet sneeze.

A couple who looked to be around 80 and a young girl approached. "How do ya do," the man greeted Lucy with a gracious smile and a nod of his head. I'm Henry Ferguson, this is my wife, Mildred, and this beauty is our grandbaby, Mary. Would you have a spot for a small trailer for a week?"

Shaking Henry's extended hand, Lucy returned the smile. "I'm Lucy, the campground manager. I'm sure we can find a nice spot for you. Loop C has some nice shady spots available, if that sounds good."

Mary, meanwhile, had spotted Sassy. "Oh, look at the pretty doggy! Can I pet her, please?" Her large blue eyes appealed to the three adults until the right one gave the right answer.

"I believe Sassy would really like that, Mary. If it's all right with your grandparents."

Mildred took a seat in one of the easy chairs in the book corner and watched Mary gently pat Sassy's head.

Yup, Sassy's my name and charm's my game. Come on girls, go for it! Rub-a-dub-dub!

"Me-maw, can I have a dog like this? Look how nice she is!" Sassy had moved closer to Mildred's chair. She rolled onto her back, roping both Mary and Mildred into a belly-rub.

"Maybe someday, Mary, when you're old enough to take it for walks and care for it yourself. You know your Papaw and me are gettin' too old for all that."

"But I'm six, Me-maw, almost seven! I'm old enough now, honest. I'll do extra chores and help buy the food and take the best care of it you ever saw."

"Keep it down, Mary, and listen to your Me-maw," interrupted Henry. "I'm trying to concentrate here. Okay, Miss Lucy, you say that will be $30 a night? Do you give a discount for old folks or for a week's stay?"

"No, sir, I'm sorry. But we do discount the monthly rate to $600, plus electric."

"Nice place, ma'am, but we don't need to be here a month. Have a ranch to get back to." Henry chuckled and counted out a handful of bills.

Equipped with a packet of information, the trio left for the site Lucy had recommended in Loop C. Mary looked longingly over her shoulder. She blew Sassy a kiss with her free hand, letting her grandmother lead her out the door with the other.

Being a slow Thursday, the next guests did not arrive until two hours had passed. They could not have been more different from the previous little family.

Crisply marching to Lucy's counter, the man snapped out his credit card and the woman began rattling off their reservation number and firing off questions. Not even a simple "hello" prefaced the onslaught.

"Do you have activities for the children?" she asked, gesturing to a girl and a boy who had started chasing Sassy around the store. They looked to be a little older than Mary.

"Chester, Tiffany, not so fast... You might slip and fall!"

Help, Mom, help! These kids are wackadoodle!

"Over here, girl," Lucy beckoned. She smiled at the two children and adroitly blocked their attempt to follow Sassy to her refuge behind the counter.

Certain that Sassy was safely settled into her bed, Lucy returned her attention to the parents, who had started bickering.

"I *told* you we should have..."

"You *never* said..."

"If only *once* you'd..."

"It's not *my* fault you..."

Lucy interrupted, a little more shrilly than she intended. "WELCOME to Sherwood Forest Campground. I'm sorry, but no, we do not have any organized activities for the children. There is a small playground in the center of each of our four camping loops, though. There is a trail between B and C loops in the rear of the campground that connects to many miles of hiking trails in the national forest, which we border." She pulled a map out of their packet. "Over here is a lake with a swimming beach that's on national forest land that the children might enjoy. It's only 10 miles away."

"Are there alligators in it?" asked Chester, running up to the counter, his sister close on his heels. "I don't want to go swimming with no alligators!"

"There ain't no alligators in Texas, you dummy. They all live in Florida!" Tiffany smacked her brother on the back of his head.

The closer she looked, Lucy realized they were probably twins, maybe around eight years old. Looking up at Lucy sweetly, Tiffany announced, "That's where *we're* from. Florida. It's full of alligators and their favorite meal is BOYS," she screamed the last word into Chester's ear.

Lucy left the subject of alligator habitat and dietary preferences for the parents to sort out later and concentrated on the check-in process, speeding it up as much as possible.

The Davis family—Ron and Gloria and their eight-year old twins, Chester and Tiffany—were then sent on their way to Loop D, which had several sites large enough for their 38-foot fifth-wheel trailer. Wade, the maintenance man, also resided in Loop D and could help them get into their site, if needed. Lucy suspected help would indeed be needed.

After they left, Lucy bent down and gave Sassy a quick pat on the head. "Whew, that was a tough one, girl. I think it's time for a good walk and some fresh air. Heck, we might even pack it up early today. I'm beat."

Sassy snorted her approval and grabbed her leash from next to her bed. Such a smart dog.

Lucy... Jack

The old wall clock mounted above the office door limped along to five o'clock, one hour before official closing. Lucy struggled to stay awake, despite a nice exercise break with

Sassy. No one had come in since the Davis family. The phone hadn't even rung.

Free to nap, Sassy did so.

Lucy began totaling the day's receipts using an adding machine from the last century. It was her favorite piece of office equipment. She loved the feel of the buttons when she entered the data and chuckled at the odd cranking noise it made when she hit "enter." Most of all, she appreciated the ink-on-paper result. It was all so concrete compared to the mysterious, sterile workings of modern cellular, cyber, and cloud devices, all of which she judged to be beyond untrustworthy in comparison. Heavens to Betsy, she thought, what would one do if all the modern contraptions went kaput? If the cloud burst, the net sported a big hole, a giant spider invaded the web, Alexa contracted a virus? Revert back to the basics? Add two and two in the head? Barely a soul would know what to do. She chuckled to herself, realizing that some of the most valuable people in such a crisis might be the old ones. The ones who remembered how to actually *do* things.

The door jingled, interrupting Lucy's reverie. Sassy lazily opened one eye.

"Ah, what a beautiful sight," rang a familiar voice. Sassy's ears perked. Her other eye opened. Her nose snuffed. Before Lucy could reply, Sassy was on the run, eager to greet their good friend. Finding his scruffy, four-legged guardian in the way, she tackled him instead.

Bo! What are you doing here, boy? What a surprise... Woo Hooo! Come on everybody, let's go for a walk! Play ball!! Have a cook-out!!! Oh! Hotdogs and hamburgers!!!!

If she had pants on, Sassy would have peed in them. As it was, she barely managed to maintain control while wrestling little Bo to the ground. She was very conscious of proper behavior where it most counted, but not much beyond.

Looking back and forth from the dogs to her friend, Lucy grinned speechlessly.

Finally finding her voice, "Jack! What are you doing here? And all the way from Tennessee! Why didn't you let me know you were coming?" She came out from behind the counter, stepped around the wrestling dogs, and gave their friend a hug.

"Hello, Lucy! Bo and I wanted to surprise you." Jack kissed Lucy lightly on the cheek, then pointed out the front window. "Look! I bought a small Airstream trailer. It's an old one, but a solid classic. Ed and Trixie helped me make sure it was in good shape and then helped smooth out a few rough edges when I got it home. This is our maiden voyage and, honestly, I'm just glad we made it. Highway driving and campground parking with this thing has been a challenge."

Ed was Jack's older brother and Trixie was Ed's bride of less than a year. They were in their mid-70's and lived on Ed's old family farm south of Nashville. They often camped at Sunny Acres, Lucy's campground in east Tennessee. Trixie was a good friend of Lucy's and had introduced Jack to her at Sunny Acres a few months ago. It had been quite an introduction.

Jack continued, "Bo and I figured your campground would be a good spot to enjoy some winter warmth mixed with Texas hospitality. We'd like a site for a couple of weeks if you have any openings."

"Well, I hope we have enough of that warmth you're looking for. It can still get pretty chilly in this part of Texas, especially at night. Let's see what we have available. Hmmm..." Lucy had returned to her station behind the counter. She clickety-clacked at the computer keyboard. A little too hard. A little too long. Her racing brain and her beating heart interfered with her fingers' attempt to function normally. *Stupid fingers.*

"Here we go," she finally announced. "Number 18 in Loop B is free for a solid two weeks. It's one of the prettiest sites in the campground. Nice and quiet in the back corner, surrounded by big, shady pines." Lucy showed Jack on the campground map how to get there from the office, then rang up his credit card for the two-week fee.

"Thanks, Lucy." Jack collected his receipt, his fingers lingering long enough to give Lucy's a warm squeeze before retreating. "I can't guarantee a spread like Trixie puts on, but Bo and I would sure like to share some hotdogs and a can of beans with a couple of walking buddies... Say, 7:00 or so?" He had taken note of the 6:00 closing time posted on the office door when he had entered.

At the mention of hotdogs, Sassy left Bo prostrate and panting from their wrestling match and leapt onto Jack, nearly knocking him over. Sassy wasn't a huge dog—at best guess, she was a small lab mix—but she was powerful, and hotdogs were one of her favorite sources of fuel.

"Sure," Lucy laughed. "We'll be there with bells on. Let me know if you need any help setting up and I'll send Wade over. He's our maintenance guru and is very good at navigating trailers into their spots if you have any trouble."

"Thanks, yes, I've been getting some practice between Tennessee and Texas, but help is always welcome. See you later, then."

Lucy watched them go from the office window. Jack gave Bo a boost into their truck and then carefully headed to B-18 with their brand new-to-them silver trailer. It sure was pretty. And shiny. Bo sure looked healthy. And happy. And Jack... well, Jack looked great. Lucy could just kick herself for feeling so... so sappy.

Lucy picked up the office phone and called Wade. Unlike Sunny Acres, which was part of the Tennessee State Park system, Sherwood Forest Campground was privately owned and operated. That meant more leeway when it came to operations and appearances.

Wade was the owner's younger brother and his job, his livelihood, the enormity of his whole, simple life was largely contained within the campground boundaries. He and his little dog, Ginger, occupied the last site in Loop D, next to the maintenance building. Unlike Lucy, who was there from December to March, and the camp hosts who helped out anywhere from one to three months at a time in exchange for a free site, Wade lived there year-round in an old trailer that probably couldn't be moved without the help of a crane. He only left for a few hours once a week in his beat-up Ford pickup, presumably to get groceries and take care of whatever other necessities may be pressing.

Lucy wasn't sure exactly what his issues were, but Wade's appearance and behavior made an initial impression that was confusing and could be off-putting, until you got to know him, which took time because he kept pretty much to himself. Lucy came to know him gradually through working together every winter for the last five years, but their best visits were at the campground's dog park while Sassy and Ginger ran free and played.

Regular visitors grew to appreciate Wade for his mechanical skill when things went wrong with their RVs. New guests, however, generally viewed his full-bearded, long-haired, scrawny figure—usually clad in pink-&-camo accents—with great skepticism. In all honesty, Lucy could see their point. At first glance. But Wade was a solid worker and his mechanical prowess was a priceless asset. More importantly, Lucy could tell from their dog park visits that he had a huge heart and a gentle soul.

"Wade? Hey. It's Lucy. We have a guest— actually a friend of mine from Tennessee— putting a vintage Airstream into B-18... Yeah, it can be a little tricky backing into that one and it's getting dark out. Do you mind running over to make sure he gets in okay?... Great. Thanks. Oh, and if you hang around, hotdogs and beans are on the menu after he sets up... Yes, I'll drop in, too. With a salad and maybe some wine... Absolutely, bring Ginger... Okay, I'll see you later, and thanks."

Lucy quickly wrapped up business for an early closing, grateful for the extra time—she couldn't believe she was thinking this—to pretty-up as best she could.

A Pause

A million questions were trampling all over Sassy's effort to be patient. Why was Mom wasting all this time when their good buddies were somewhere close by? Why did she keep trying on different clothes until finally picking something so frilly and bright? She never wore that skirt before... where had it even come from? Where were her pants? Where was she going to hang her keys? And why was she messing around so much with her hair? Wasn't she going to wear her campground cap? How would everyone know she was the boss without her cap and her jingling keys?

Sassy nudged Lucy's knee with a very wet nose.

Come on, Mom, hurry up! Before Bo eats all the hotdogs!

"Settle down, girl, you will be richly rewarded for your patience." Lucy put the finishing touch, a purple ribbon, onto her long side braid. She scratched Sassy's ear then hooked the leash to her harness, grabbed her keys, and finally headed for the door, grabbing a big paper bag from the counter on the way. Sassy could smell kibble in there, further feeding her impatience.

Before they made it to the door, there came a loud knocking from the other side. Lucy immediately opened it, almost hitting Mr. Davis in the face. She led Sassy outside and around the large man, who had retreated two steps. Mr. Davis stood there alone, his arms tightly folded, feet solidly planted, mouth firmly set.

"Mr. Davis. What can I do for you?" Lucy put the paper bag into the back of the EZ-Go work cart and returned to her trailer to lock the door.

"Yes, well, my wife and I have some concerns we want to bring to your attention. There is a man living in a shabby looking trailer across from us and, well, we assume he works here or something. He offered to help us get into our site, which was not needed... You do know we have small children. We want to know if you do background checks on all of your employees."

"That would be Wade you are referring to and, yes, he has worked here for many years. Has he done something that concerns you?" Lucy invited Sassy onto the EZ-Go's bench seat then climbed in next to her. She put the key into the ignition.

"Well, no, not yet, but my wife is not comfortable having the children exposed to someone so... um..."

Lucy waited quietly while Mr. Davis struggled to find his next words.

"You see, Ma'am, I am the pastor of the Church of the Blessed Children of the Almighty and Everlasting Army of God..."

"The Church of the what?"

Sassy whined.

"The Church of the Blessed Children of the Almighty and Everlasting Army of God." Mr. Davis' voice lowered a few notes and quivered on "God." Lucy imagined his sermons must be mesmerizing. Cold, but mesmerizing.

"Are the children the children, then, of the Army or of the God?"

Mr. Davis stared blankly.

"And which is the Almighty and Everlasting, the God or the Army?"

Still no answer.

"Sorry, Mr. Davis, I'm just trying to understand. That's quite a mouthful, and I'm sure you don't want to mislead...

"You look like a fine, God-fearing woman, Ma'am. You must understand how important it is to protect our children—God's children—from the evil and confusion clouding the world of today. If the Devil himself is free to strut around like some wanton harlot and people actually celebrate the confusion..."

"Are you comparing Wade to the Devil because of the way he looks and dresses, Mr. Davis? If so, I am not aware of any background check that could ferret out such information.

Surely, he would be too tricky and skilled to be discovered by a mere bureaucratic tool. Background checks only go so deep, you know." Lucy got out of her cart and faced the man straight on. She was a tall woman and met him eye-to-eye. He retreated a step.

Sassy shifted to Lucy's seat and emitted a low growl. Part of it came from a place deep in her throat, the other part from her stomach.

Mom! What are you doing? We have places to go. Friends to see. Food to eat. Where are your priorities? Don't waste time with this guy. I don't have a good feeling about him, and you know I am an expert judge of character.

Lucy continued. "Nevertheless, I will pass your concerns along to the owner of the campground, Jeremy Ogletree. He will get in touch with you tomorrow. Meanwhile, if you would like to have a different site, we may be able to accommodate that request in the morning. The office opens at 11:00. Right now, I have other things to attend to. Good night, Mr. Davis."

Sassy scooted back to her side of the bench. Lucy slid in, started the EZ-Go, and drove off for their date, leaving Mr. Davis scowling in their dusty fumes.

A Gathering

"*BO!!!*" Sassy leapt from the work cart while it was still moving and tackled the shaggy gray pup before he saw what hit him. Poor Ginger, the smallest of the three, almost got trampled. She held her own, though, as tiny dogs tend to do, barking furiously at both Bo and Sassy and nipping at their heels.

"Sassy! Get back here, you fur-ball!" Sassy skulked back to her mistress, who took hold of her leash, patted her on the head, and led her back over to Bo and Ginger in a more dignified fashion.

Tied to the same tree, the pups lavished love and play until they were inextricably wrapped around one another and the tree. Unable to move any farther, the threesome lay down in a pile, snouts between front paws. *Silly humans*, they panted in unison, watching Lucy venture into her own evening's entanglements.

"Hello, Jack. Hey, Wade." She put a bottle of wine and a bowl of spinach salad onto the picnic table next to a steaming pot of baked beans, a bag of chips, and a container of dip. Wade nodded at Lucy. He dipped a chip with one hand and slugged a beer with the other. His long, auburn hair was done up in a French braid—something Lucy had never been able to pull off—and adorned with a bright pink ribbon about halfway down his back. The braid was longer and the ribbon brighter than Lucy's. She always had to fight her jealousy of Wade's long, thick mane. He wore pale yellow leggings under an oversized, long-sleeved, camo t-shirt. She wished her legs looked half as good.

Jack came over from tending hotdogs on the fire and gave Lucy a quick peck on the cheek. "Lucy, salad, wine! Perfect!" He opened the bottle, poured each of them a glass, then turned to Wade and his bottle of beer.

"Salute, Wade. Thanks for your help getting me into this spot." Turning to Lucy: "And cheers to this lovely lady for inspiring me to take off on this journey in the first place."

Lucy blushed. "I did no such thing. If you got bit by some wanderlust bug, I had nothing to do with that."

"Au contraire, my dear. I figured if a woman as delicate and lovely as you..."

Lucy snorted.

"... could pursue a life on the road on her own these last ten years..."

"Twelve," Lucy corrected.

"... twelve years, oh my. All the more reason for me find a way to follow my own long-held vagabond dream."

The three clinked drinks and Jack headed back to the campfire. Like silent stalkers from the forest deep, three sets of dog eyes followed his every move. Three noses twitched with each splatter of hotdog grease that hit the fire. Imaginations ran—amazingly in-sync with one another—through the darkness of the trees, pretending to be on a mighty hunt for the Great Hotdog Beast. Bo flipped onto his back and nipped Sassy's ear. She ignored him. Ginger started to snore.

Lucy took a seat across from Wade, placing a paper napkin onto the bench before sitting down. "Wow, you sure did get set up fast for a newbie, Jack. House all settled *and* dinner on the table!" Lucy looked around, admiring how stable and level the trailer was. Awnings, welcome mat, and camp chairs were all deployed. Even a bicycle was out, leaning against the back of Jack's truck.

"Sure did, but let's give credit where credit is due. Wade built the fire while I unpacked all my stuff. Better yet, he is a genius and a terrific teacher," Jack smiled. "It took no time at all backing into this site with his help. He explained things so well that the next time I face a 90-degree angle in the dark, I can handle it on my own."

"Well, I'm impressed. I know I couldn't do it. That's why I drove a small motorhome rather than towing a trailer for so many years. I didn't even tow a car. You're going to have to give me some lessons before my trip back to Tennessee this spring, Wade. I still have a heck of a time maneuvering my trailer into some spots." Wade nodded and smiled without quite meeting Lucy's eyes, as was his norm.

"Hotdogs are ready," Jack announced, approaching the table with a sizzling pan. "Sorry, but no condiments. Just buns and beans. And thanks for the chips, Wade, and the salad, Lucy. Looks like there's plenty to go around. Let's dig in!"

Sassy licked Bo's ear and the two dogs joined Ginger in her sweet dreams, confident that when their turn came, they would not be forgotten. Even so, they each kept one eyelid cracked and on those hotdogs.

A Campfire

Sassy and Bo were sleeping off their feast under the tree. Lucy, Jack, and Wade sat around a roaring campfire, glasses in hand. Wade's tongue had loosened around the four-beer count. Really loosened.

"I just want someone who can love me like my dog. Is that too much to ask?" Ginger was settled into Wade's lap, belly up, eyes half-closed, tongue dangling out of the side of her snout. Daddy was giving her a belly-rub.

"Of course not," Lucy replied. "That's what anyone in their right mind wishes."

"Or is it?" Jack speculated. "I mean, our dogs—wonderful as they are—can still only love us to a certain point, if you get my drift..."

"Drift, pfffft. You know good and well what I'm saying. Physicalities aside, there is absolutely nothing—unless you are blessedly lucky—that approaches the standard of love that our dogs give to us. I think there are a few, a minority of couples who may find that with each other. Who can treat each other with empathy and work through the challenges of this world, our society, the simple day-to-day give and take, and still hold onto... mutual adoration. *Adoration.* That's it. My Sassy adores me, and I adore her."

"Well, my Bo *worships—*"

"THERE you are! What kind of a place IS this?" Gloria Davis strode into the circle of firelight, shattering the friendly gathering's energy as if the full moon had exploded into a billion brightly ragged stars and rained down upon on their heads. She stopped in front of

Lucy, boney hands clasping ample hips, stomping Jack's reply into mid-sentence smoke.

"I couldn't find you at the site posted on the office door. It was just luck that I saw you sitting here," she spat. Her fiery gaze flickered past Lucy and settled on Wade's pink bow and colorful attire.

"How can I help you, Mrs. Davis?" Lucy rose from her seat and placed herself between the distraught woman and Wade.

"It's Tiffany. I can't find her. She and Chester were up by *this* one's trailer a bit ago..." She gestured towards Wade. "I called them back from there, then I went in to clean up after dinner. When Chester came in, he was alone. He said the last he saw of his sister, she was running off with that little Mary girl to go hunt for alligators."

"Did you check at Mary's campsite? Did you ask her grandparents, Mildred and Henry Ferguson?" Lucy put her arm around the woman's bony shoulders. Jack rose and stood slightly back from the two women. Wade vacated his seat and carried Ginger over to the other two dogs. He crouched down and scratched their ears, just outside the circle of firelight.

"I don't know what site they are on!" Mrs. Davis practically screamed.

Jack interrupted, "Where is your husband? Is he out looking for Tiffany?"

Mrs. Davis sniffed and averted her eyes. "He is taking his after-dinner nap and I do not want to disturb him unless absolutely necessary. The children are my responsibility."

Lucy guided Gloria Davis to the work cart. Looking over her shoulder, she called, "Keep an eye on Sassy for me, will you guys? I'll be back in a bit."

"Let us know how we can help, once you get more information, Lucy," replied Jack.

"Will do." Lucy fired up the little engine and took off with a jolt. Mrs. Davis had to hold onto the hand grip with both hands while Lucy sped through the campground to the Ferguson's trailer.

It didn't take long to get there. Sherwood Forest only had four small camping loops, each with 12 sites. The store/office, laundromat, and bathhouse were in the center of the campground, and each of the camping loops ran off from the center ring like four petals of a flower. Everything was compact, and children easily migrated from loop to loop to play and explore. Lucy sent up a silent prayer that they would find Tiffany in Loop C.

A Painful Pause

Tiffany and Mary giggled wildly while roasting marshmallows over the Ferguson's campfire. Henry and Mildred relaxed nearby in their camp chairs. They smiled broadly when Lucy and Tiffany's mother pulled up. Smiles melted and laughter dissolved at the look on Mrs. Davis' face.

"Tiffany!" She leapt from the work cart before Lucy had set the brake. "Oh, baby, what are you doing here? I didn't know where you were! Why didn't you tell me?" She clasped poor Tiffany to her bony breast.

"I told Chester to tell you, Mom," Tiffany managed to squeak out from between her mother's spastic hugs.

The Fergusons quickly approached.

"Oh, my," exclaimed Mildred, "I am so sorry! I thought y'all knew where Tiffany was. I am so sorry!"

"Please, ma'am, we didn't mean no harm," added Henry. "Just a quick marshmallow roast, then we were gonna walk your girl back ourselves. Her brother, he said he would let y'all know where his sister was at."

Tiffany buried her head into her mother's neck and wrapped her legs around her waist. Mrs. Davis struggled to rise. Henry reached out to assist.

"Thank you, no harm done, I am sure. Let me just get my daughter safely back home and settle her down. Good night." Once vertical, Mrs. Davis awkwardly marched back to Lucy's cart and sat down with Tiffany firmly set upon her lap.

Lucy turned to the Fergusons. "I am so sorry. I'm sure it was a simple misunderstanding and that all will be well in the morning."

"Will Tiffany be allowed to come play with me again?" Mary peeked out from behind her Me-maw's skirts.

Lucy knelt down and faced the girl. "We'll see, ladybug. But don't you worry about it.

You and your grandparents are gonna have the best time camping here ever."

"Can I play some more with Sassy, Miss Lucy?"

"You betcha. Sassy loves little girls. You come on over to the office any time your grandparents say it's ok." Lucy gave Mary's hand a reassuring squeeze.

Looking over her shoulder at Gloria and Tiffany Davis, she addressed the Fergusons, "I have to get these two back to their site. Y'all gonna be ok?" She rose and turned back to the elderly couple, who were standing arm in arm.

"Don't worry about us, Miss Lucy," said Henry. "Just take good care of 'em and we'll see you tomorrow."

"Have a good night, dear," Mildred added.

Henry wrapped his arm around his wife's waist and gave her a warm kiss on the cheek. He took Mary's hand in his free hand and led his two beloved ladies back to their camper.

Lucy returned to the EZ-Go, fired it up, and drove off much more slowly than the manner in which they had arrived. She dropped her passengers off at their trailer, waited until they closed their door, then drove back to Jack's site. Wade and Ginger had already left. Exhausted, Lucy stayed just long enough to report that all was well, then gather up Sassy and their things and head home.

Lying in bed that night, imagination triumphed over exhaustion. Lucy tossed and turned for a couple of hours, her mind waging almighty battle with her heart. When sleep finally came, her dreams continued in the theme of her waking hours: Jack. What to do about Jack.

Sassy slept like a log. Or a dog. No difference in this case.

Longings

Jeremy Ogletree—Lucy's boss and Wade's older brother—came in from town to talk to Mr. and Mrs. Davis first thing in the morning. He must have offered the proper assurances. Rather than leaving, they moved from Loop D to Loop B, two sites down from Jack's trailer. It turned out to be a long, drawn-out affair given the size of their RV and all of their gear. Jack enjoyed watching them navigate into their new spot while sipping his morning coffee. Even with Jeremy's help, it took well over an hour to get their rig safely backed in, level, and hooked up to utilities.

Jeremy stayed until they were all settled. By then it was lunch time, and he left to meet with Lucy at the camp store/office.

"I swear," Lucy said, handing him a steaming cup of coffee, "those people have caused more upset in one day than most guests can accomplish in a month. Did you set their minds at ease about Wade?"

"Don't worry about all that, Lucy, they seem to be happy enough for now. As for you, you deserve a medal for what you have to put up with. You don't know how much I appreciate being able to take a break and leave this place mostly in your hands over the winter months." Jeremy sank into one of the chairs in the book corner and took an appreciative sip of his coffee. Sassy leaned against his leg and placed her head just so... He scratched her ear with his free hand.

"I couldn't do it without Wade and Diane, that's for sure."

"Speaking of Diane, where is she? I thought she was supposed to be here by now, but I didn't see her rig in the camp host site."

"Oh, her truck needed some work done so she's been delayed a few days. That's all right. She's one of the best camp hosts we've had here. She's eager to learn and is a big help to Wade with maintenance stuff, and it's great to have relief in the office for me. I'm just happy she keeps coming back year after year. I guess we're doing something right."

"Just be sure you take your time off, Lucy. I can come fill in some until Diane arrives. That little trailer behind Wade's serves me just fine for a few nights at a time. Besides, you know you can close the office any time you need to. The guests can use the self-pay station, and if they want something from the store, town is only 15 minutes away. Things are a whole lot cheaper there than in our little store anyways," he laughed.

"So, speaking of time off," Jeremy continued, tentatively, "Wade tells me you have a gentleman friend who followed you all the way down from Tennessee. I spotted him this morning over by his sweet little Airstream. He seemed to be well entertained watching the Davis family move in. Are you planning to show him the local sights?" Jeremy's brown eyes twinkled.

"My goodness! Isn't your brother the gossip," Lucy laughed. She left her seat by Jeremy and returned to the office counter, trying to hide the silly hot blush she was unable to prevent from climbing her face.

Luckily, the door jingled open and Mary skipped in, closely followed by her grandmother.

Grateful for the diversion, Lucy quickly exclaimed, "Hello there Mary, Mildred! What can we do for you today? Did you have a good night's sleep?"

Sassy ran to greet Mary, who met her half-way and gave her a big hug around her neck. Sassy was an extraordinarily gentle, patient dog and wonderful with children, a great asset in campground life.

"We slept great," responded Mildred. "Thank you! Have you heard anything more from Tiffany's folks? Is everything all right with them this morning?"

"No worries, Mildred. This is Jeremy Ogletree, by the way." Jeremy rose to shake Mildred's hand. "He's the campground owner and took care of everything this morning. The Davis family is located in Loop B now, B-16, if you want to see them."

While Mildred and Jeremy made small talk, Mary ran to the counter and jumped up and down with uncontainable excitement. "Miss Lucy! Guess what we saw! We saw a little doggy runnin' through the woods by our campsite this morning. He didn't have no collar or nothin' so I think he's lost and needs a home. We couldn't catch him, though. Papaw tried real hard. He tossed him a piece of bacon, and the dog ran up and grabbed it quick as lightnin', but Papaw was too slow to catch that dog. He is fast! Papaw says he's a hound dog. A *smart* hound dog. Arrroooo!"

Pausing for breath, Mary glanced back at her grandmother. Cupping her hands on either side of her mouth, she stood on tip-toe and whispered to Lucy: "Papaw says that if I can catch him, I can have him. But don't tell Me-maw yet."

As if on cue, Mildred turned to Lucy, "Oh, Lucy, dear, I was just telling Jeremy what a beautiful campground y'all have here. To have put a playground and a gazebo in the middle of each camping loop, well, I've never seen anything like it. And it's so nice to have a laundry room, too. Speaking of that, could you give me $5.00 worth of quarters so I don't have to bother you later this week?" She took a bill out of her small purse and handed it to Lucy. Mary had returned to the book corner and was sitting on the floor petting Sassy.

The door jingled open and Jack entered, Bo trotting alongside. It was a race to see who got to the pup first, Sassy or Mary. In either case, Jack was surrounded and could not take another step.

Before the door had quite closed, Wade walked in. He looked at all the people and almost ran right back out, but his brother stopped him.

"Wade, great!" Jeremy called. "Lucy is taking a couple of days off, so stick around for a bit and we can talk about what needs to be done. Lucy," he said, turning back to her surprised face, "before you go, be a sweetheart and print me off a list of arrivals and departures for today and tomorrow. Then, please, go. Have a great time. I love you, but I don't want to see you before Sunday morning." He eyed Jack, who was still trying to untangle himself from two dogs and a little girl.

Lucy, for all of her years, had finally learned when it was best not to argue.

After a quick lunch, she and Jack were riding through the east Texas countryside, truck windows wide open, one happy dog head sticking out of each rear window, tongues and ears flapping in the breeze.

Freedom

Over the next two days, Sassy watched her Mom turn from a serious, somewhat stiff old woman into a giggling, starry-eyed young girl. Well, maybe not young. You could only stretch things so far. But starry-eyed, yeah, for sure. Unfortunately, when they were alone back in their trailer at night, Lucy would do an about-face and fret over her growing feelings for Jack, questioning whether or not she was doing the right thing.

Sassy picked up on these conflicting emotions, partly because she was a very sensitive dog and partly because her Mom talked to herself out loud all the time. Humans could be so wonderful, but they had a weird tendency to overthink things. Why make life more complicated than it really was?

It was really quite simple, in Sassy's view. Her Mom and Jack had met back in Tennessee, and here he was, showing up out of the blue... something must have attracted him. They got along great, sharing lots of great walks and talks, holding hands, touching lips-to-cheeks now and then. Best yet, their dog companions loved each other no end.

What more do you want? Get on with it, already!

At least, that's how Sassy saw it.

Never one to stew too long over any one thing, Sassy had other matters on her mind that distracted her from her Mom's concerns.

The little hound that Mary had spoken of returned to the campground daily, begging scraps off of campers yet avoiding all attempts at capture. Sassy and Bo encountered him a few times while walking the campground loops with Lucy and Jack. Nothing could tempt him close enough to be caught.

Sassy had had her own bad experiences before being rescued by Lucy (two blessed years ago, at the ripe old age of ten) and understood the pup's struggles well. He was desperate for food, yet he even more desperately feared the food giver. Quite the conundrum.

Sassy and Bo tried to entice the little hound to follow along when they met him on their walks. He would give lively chase for a little while, running in and out, nipping at their heels then tearing back out of reach, teasing: *Ha, look at me... I am free!*

Sassy didn't have the heart to point out to him that some freedoms weren't all they were cracked up to be. And some ties were more wonderful than snuggling up with a soup bone under a woolen blanket on a snowy winter night. That was the kind of thing you only believed once you discovered it for yourself.

So, she waited. And she watched. She noticed that the pup gravitated towards the back of the campground, behind the dog park, where the campground trail began. She wasn't sure just what she was waiting for, but she had a sense that something important was approaching.

Sassy smelled danger, and she had a very good nose.

Danger

Mildred Ferguson pushed the front door open so vigorously that it nearly knocked over one of the store's display racks. Totally out of character, she didn't even notice.

"Lucy, oh, Lucy, we can't find Mary!"

It was Sunday morning, a big day for departures. Lucy, fresh from two days off, had opened the office a short while ago.

"How long has she been gone? Where did you last see her?" Lucy dropped her paperwork and ran to Mildred, Sassy close on her heels. The two women clasped hands. The dog sat patiently at their feet, her ears perked.

"She went outside to play after breakfast. Maybe 9:00 or so. Henry said he last saw her through the window before he took a shower around 10:00. She was playing at the picnic table with her dolls."

"That's an hour and a half ago, honey. Y'all haven't seen her since then?"

"Oh, God forgive us, Henry and me were enjoying a nice slow Sunday morning. Mary's such a good child. We couldn't imagine that she might run off. Or... Oh, Lucy, could someone have taken her? There's a lot of rigs that pulled out today already."

The pit in Lucy's stomach started to bubble and burn. "No, honey, don't even go there. Maybe she went to Tiffany's... Where is Henry? Is he out looking for her?"

"Oh, yes. Right before I came over he came back from walking all four campground loops to tell me that he didn't find her. And, yes, he checked with the Davis family. They haven't seen her either. He came back to send me to tell you what's going on and then went right back out to look for her some more."

"Here, hon', sit down." Lucy led Mildred to one of the book corner easy chairs, gave her a cup of water, then went over the office phone. "Sit tight. I'm calling Jeremy and Wade."

Jeremy had not returned to his place in town yet and was still at Wade's. He arrived within a few minutes.

No one noticed Sassy slip out the door when he barged in.

He rushed to the two women holding hands, talking in the book corner. After verifying the timeline since Mary's disappearance and efforts to find her, he called the Sheriff's department. By then it was a little after noon, two hours since Mary had last been seen.

Jeremy had just hung up the phone when Henry walked in. Mr. Davis was close behind. Mildred flew into Henry's arms.

"Anything, dear? Have you found anything that shows where Mary might have gone?" Mildred was having a hard time holding back sobs.

Henry gathered his wife into his arms. "We'll find her, honey. She's probably off somewhere playing or exploring. Don't worry." Henry stroked Mildred's hair; her head rested on his chest. He looked to Lucy. "Jack joined me in the search and is still out looking for her. He's knocking on all the campers' doors to see if anyone has seen her, including the ones in the process of pulling out."

Mr. Davis stepped up from the background and cleared his throat. "Gloria and the children are home praying for Mary. The good Lord will surely take care of your sweet, innocent granddaughter until she can be found." Glancing sideways at Lucy as if to make sure she was at a safe distance, he continued. "I was wondering if anyone has checked into that handyman's trailer... You know, just in case Mary decided to visit there for some reason..."

The question hung in the air for a tenuous moment. Jeremy looked ready to explode. Lucy's mouth opened as if to reply, but no words came to her. Raw nerves traveled through the group like an errant electrical current... The door jingled and everyone jumped. Wade entered. He immediately felt pained by the heavy, emotional energy clouding the room.

The shrill, blasting pulse of police sirens soon shattered the uneasy silence. Two cars pulled up, and Wade held the door open for four officers to join the group in the office. It was getting uncomfortably crowded.

Sassy, meanwhile, had made straight for the trail at the rear of the campground. The one that led into the vast wilderness of the national forest.

Darkness

Sassy quickly caught the hound pup's scent. Shortly after, she found that of the little girl. The two sometimes ran together and sometimes diverged.

They had left the trail behind and traveled deep into the forest, crossing small creeks and climbing up and down many hills. The tracks became confusing in spots, seeming to run in circles. Other animals had crossed the tracks here and there, including some with smells that Sassy didn't recognize.

Sassy often lost both scents entirely and, as the afternoon wore on, the tracks became even harder to follow. At one very discouraging point, she noticed a small, golden light—like a tiny candle flame—pop up to her left. It swayed from side to side. When she went to investigate, she was able to relocate the scents. Meanwhile, the light moved ahead. Sassy followed. And so did the scents, the light and the scents now seeming to track together.

But Sassy was getting up there in years and, after a while, she had to slow her pace in order to keep going at all. The light slowed to match.

I sure wish Bo was here. He may have short legs, but he's got more stamina than I ever had, even when I was his age. I bet he's taking a nap right now. I sure could use a nap... and some lunch... and some company. I wonder what that light is, anyways. Funny, it has no smell...

Sassy shook off her thoughts and refocused on her task. She stopped to drink from a small stream then sat perfectly still. Nose, ears, eyes, all on hyperalert, scanned the surrounding terrain.

She noticed that the ground upstream from her position looked a bit strange and went to examine it more closely. An area nearly the size of the campground office had been torn up into pits and chunks, as if some animal had dug it up with its powerful snout. Upon closer examination, Sassy guessed it was at least a dozen such animals. Their smell was strong. And wild. And scary. She wondered if that was what bear smelled like.

Sassy returned to Mary's tracks and resumed her hunt, pushing through creeping exhaustion and a growing ache in her limbs. She found encouragement in that golden light, bobbing and racing ahead of her, becoming larger and glowing more brightly as the darkness deepened.

*

"Sassy wouldn't just run off for no reason. She's such a smart dog. Faithful, loyal. I just know she went after Mary."

It was early evening. Spirits and hopes were fading as quickly as the day's light. Jack and Lucy were in his trailer with Mildred and Henry, sharing a small dinner—which nobody had appetite for—and comparing notes on the day. Jeremy and Wade were in the office, helping the Sheriff's department set up a makeshift command center.

"You're probably right," replied Jack, "but how are we going to find either of them? The sheriff's deputies have had no luck here in the campground. They're following up with the campers who left earlier—before we knew Mary was missing—tracking them down for questioning. They're bringing in a bloodhound team tomorrow morning and at first light they plan to head into the forest."

"A few of the campers here want to help with the search, too," Lucy added. "Wade is organizing them. He is really stepping out of his comfort zone to do it."

"Bloodhound team... Morning... That's so far away." Mildred's voice was faint and flat.

"Well, in my opinion, they'll be following a cold trail already blazed by my Sassy. If we could find her, then I know we'd find Mary."

"Wait a minute," Jack looked from Lucy to Bo to Lucy again. "Bo can help us. I know he's still young, but he has good sense and a great nose. And he adores Sassy. What do you think? Want to take a walk and see what happens?"

Lucy didn't even respond. She just put her sneakers back on while Jack attached Bo to his harness and leash. He grabbed a flashlight for each of them and located a backpack into which he put spare batteries, a small first aid kit, matches, a box of crackers, two packages of cheese, and several bottles of water. Lucy added a few apples and a small blanket from the back of Jack's couch.

They exchanged hugs and encouraging words with Mildred and Henry, then the trio set off into the deepening night, Bo in the lead.

A Name

Mary found her pup. Or, rather, her pup found Mary.

The little hound had easily kept ahead of the girl throughout her chase. There was no reason he could not have just run ahead, full speed, putting miles between himself and his pursuer. No reason, except a nagging sense that she needed him to stay nearby. She was so small. So clumsy, compared to himself. Probably harmless, except for the fact that she obviously wanted to possess him, something in which he had no interest.

He was surprised she kept following him. He had left the human-built trail early, hoping she would give up and return to her people. But, no, she worked her way through brush and bramble, up and down hillsides. She waded through small streams, keeping her eyes on him all the while. Her small voice gently called after him: "Here boy, come to me, sweet puppy... I won't hurt you."

He began to admire the girl for her tenacity. He began to enjoy the chase, as if it were a game with another pup. He started to let her get close enough to almost touch him, then would dash off in a circle, bidding her to resume chase. And she always did.

As the sun continued to fall from its zenith, however, the girl started to trail far behind. Not for lack of effort, or of will. He could tell that her reserves were simply running out, like what happened to the rabbits he loved to chase for hours.

She began to trip on tree roots. She began to trip on her own feet. Twice, she lost her footing and tumbled down a hillside. Once, she slipped on a stone and fell to her knees in a streambed. But she never cried out, like some children he had come across, who seemed to love the screech of their own voices above all else. In fact, she seemed to be so tired that she wasn't calling to him much at all now.

Late afternoon wore on. Shadows lengthened. A damp chill set in. The pup noticed that the girl had few of the funny coverings humans generally wore. She had started the chase when the sun was high and warm. Now she shivered by a deeply shaded stream, drinking water she scooped with her hands.

The pup approached the girl carefully. He sat beside her and waited.

After drinking her fill, she reached out and softly touched his shoulder.

He steeled himself.

She shivered.

He did not move.

She wrapped her small arm around his back then drew her knees beneath her chin, clasping them close to her with her other arm.

"Well, Boo-Bear, I think we are lost. But don't worry. I'll take care of you. Oh, and you can call me Mary." She patted him gently.

The pup's heart began to melt. He had a name... and so did she.

Boo-Bear moved closer to Mary's side to share his warmth as best as he could.

Midnight Magic

The glow had grown to the size of a small ball of fire. At its center lingered the shape of an elegant black dog, laced with the whiteness of age.

Sassy, being a practical sort, did not question what she saw, even if it did appear extraordinary. Besides, she had no time for idle, philosophical questions, such as whether or not she had lost her sanity. She had stumbled into a group of wild pigs. She recognized their smell from the patch of pitted, deeply gashed earth earlier.

The largest of the pigs sported sharp, dangerous tusks. Although they weren't much taller than Sassy, they outweighed her many times over. There were young ones in the group, as well, aggravating the already aggressive nature of the adults. She wished they *were* just a bear.

Sassy had stopped cold when she saw the first pig, but it was too late. She had stumbled into their overnight shelter.

Through her initial surprise-turned-to-shock-turned-to-terror, Sassy heard a whisper of an echo:

Do not fear. Back up slowly. Relax. Hackles down, no eye contact. Slowly now, back up. It is clear behind you.

Relax, HA! Easy enough for YOU to say... They can't spear and grind a ghost into the dirt like they can me, a regular old dog. Old... Oh, GOD! I feel so old.

HUSH! Move. Do as I say.

And Sassy obeyed.

Her companion spirit dog—what else could it be?—stepped in front of Sassy, backtracking before her, step by step. The spirit's glow sent forth a wave of calm energy, putting the wild pigs at ease, until Sassy was a safe distance away.

The spirit rejoined Sassy and they quickly traced a wide arc around the wild pig encampment, shortly finding their quarry again. Sassy's heart thrilled. The scent was fresh. She had survived to smell it. And with a spirit dog, no less.

*

Lucy was lagging behind Jack, to her chagrin. They had been following Bo and his nose as quickly as they could for many hours now. But the path was hard. Heck, there was no path! They had to work their way in the dark through rough terrain. Lucy's training from her professional career—ages ago it seemed (and was)—and the years she had spent working in campgrounds helped her a great deal. But the physical limitations that accompanied age suffered no debate.

Jack's former career had also provided good training for unexpected, physically grueling circumstances. Jack followed Bo's lead through bush and bramble, regularly checking on Lucy's progress. When he and the dog got too far ahead, he pulled Bo back for a short rest. And short it was. As soon as Lucy caught up, she admonished them to get going again.

This time, however, she arrived with a slight limp.

"Lucy, sweetheart," Jack coaxed, "here, drink some water. If you don't take care of yourself, you can hardly expect to save the world."

In spite of herself, Lucy laughed. "I think that job would be better handled by dogs than humans, anyways. Bo is doing great, Jack. I can't believe he has followed Mary and Sassy's scents this far. At least I hope it's Mary and Sassy he's following..." She took a deep swig from the water bottle Jack had handed to her.

"You bet it is. This scruffy little guy has the nose of a bloodhound and the heart of a lion. It was one of the luckiest days of my life when he came into it."

Bo looked up at Jack and wagged his tail. The look in his eyes was so clear and so powerful that it nearly knocked Lucy over. Love and devotion fed the little dog's spirit, inspiring him to complete whatever task was asked of him. It didn't hurt that he loved Sassy, as well.

Lucy found a spot to sit down. Jack settled next to her. She pulled two apples from the pack and handed one to him. He took a big chunk out with his teeth and gave it to Bo before eating more himself.

"Jack..." Lucy hesitated, but only for a moment. "I just want you to know that I'm scared stiff. No, not about Mary... well, yes, about Mary... but there's more I need to say. I think I know how you feel. I'd have to be blind if I didn't after you came all this way from Tennessee. And I'd be a liar to say I didn't have feelings, too. And that's what scares me, in so many ways. Still, I want you to know that, well, I think you might be one of the best things that's come into *my* life in a very long time. No matter what happens, here, tonight, or down the road... I just want you to know that I'm really grateful for you. That's all." She took another bite from her apple, then gave the rest to Bo to chew.

Jack moved close and put his arm around Lucy. "You don't know how happy it makes me to hear that, sweetheart. As for being scared stiff, trust me, you're not alone. But the way I figure it, at our age, if we don't throw caution to the wind once in a while, then we risk that wind carrying the dust of our old bones into a very sad, very lonely place. I've been there, believe me... after Natalie died. We had been married for 40 years... knew each other since high school. Mere words cannot express how badly her death tore me up. When Ed and Trixie— well, more Trixie than Ed," he chuckled... "When they talked me into that camping trip to Sunny Acres last fall, well, to put it mildly, I was reluctant. But I went. And I met you... and something inside of me reawakened. And now? It sounds insanely simple, Lucy, but I think we should live until we die."

Lucy leaned deeply into Jack's arms. She raised her face to his. She gave and she welcomed a long, deep kiss that melted her to the core. Once there, she rediscovered the thrill of a timeless youth.

Bo looked up from his apple, watching the love story unfold. He gave them their moment, finished his apple, then set up a mighty howl.

Back to business, people! We aren't on a romantic getaway, here. C'mon, follow me!

Laughing, Lucy let Jack help her up. He made sure she was steady on her feet before giving Bo the signal, "Go, find Sassy!" Bo resumed the chase, his pace slightly slower this time in response to Jack's tug on the leash.

Reunion

Sassy finally spotted Mary and the pup a short distance ahead, resting in the light of the spirit dog's glow. They were snuggled together in a bed of pine needles, the pup wrapped around the girl, cloaking her with his limbs as much as his skinny body would allow. Exhausted, they did not stir when Sassy first approached.

She lay down, curling her warmth around the other side of Mary. The pup awoke then, but he stayed put. He seemed to fear waking the child more than he feared Sassy's intrusion into their circle. He could smell her, and he smelled friend.

The spirit dog lay down near their heads. Her entire being radiated a gentle warmth. Mary stirred, looked up at the glowing dog, and smiled knowingly before falling into a peaceful, healing rest.

Sassy fell into a deep sleep the moment she settled next to Mary. In her dreams, she addressed the beautiful spirit.

Who are you? And why do you help us?

I am the one who came before.

Riddles. Great. I really don't have the strength, patience, or talent to listen to riddles, let alone answer them. Please tell me who you are. I want to know who to thank.

I am the Midnight Unicorn. I am the guardian angel of the one you most love. And, because she most loves you, I serve you, as well.

Okaaayyy... Well, thank you for helping me. Thank you for finding Mary and the pup and for protecting us... Is there anything I can do for you in return?

Just do what you do best. Love and serve. Someday, when your end time comes, you will join me and many others, and you will continue to serve, you will continue to love.

Sassy's brain was bursting with questions, but before she could get another one out, the Midnight Unicorn began to fade.

Oh, and Sassy, one more thing.

Yes?

Thank you. Thank you for loving my Lucy.

And, poof, she was gone.

And Sassy awoke.

Sassy was about to make protest when she heard the sweetest of sounds.

"Sassy! Sassy, is that you? Yes! And look, Jack, there's Mary!"

Home

The morning sun, still too low in the sky to peer directly over the hillside, sent its rays to kiss the upper reaches of mist that covered the forest. Tiny, sparkling droplets gently cast a muted glow all the way to the forest floor from the highest peaks of the giant pines.

If you could see underneath the mist blanketing the feet of one of those pines, you would find the pup curled snug against Mary's belly, Mary cuddled back into Lucy, Lucy snuggled back to Jack, and Jack's arm holding them all close. His back was warmed by the furry ball Sassy and Bo formed, curled tightly together. It was one wild puppy pile.

Bloodhounds bayed in the distance.

"It won't be long now, ladybug," Lucy whispered, sweeping Mary's hair back from her sleepy eyes.

Jack rose, stretched, and went over to the small fire he had built the night before. Retrieving what was left of the cheese and crackers from the backpack, he cheerily announced, "Breakfast is served! Come on over, get warm. Let's get our energy up for the trip back home." He put some fresh sticks onto the fire.

"Home! Oh, Miss Lucy, I can't wait to see Me-maw and Papaw. Do you think they will like Boo-Bear?"

"What's not to like, sweetie?" Lucy finger-brushed pine needles from Mary's hair and clothing. "From what you tell me, that little guy kept you warm and safe until we got here. He's a hero dog."

"Sassy, too, Miss Lucy. And there was another dog, too. A shiny one, like an angel. Mostly black with some white mixed in, and she was glowing warm. She was gone when you got here, though. Maybe that was just a dream. Do you think so, Miss Lucy? Was it a dream?"

Lucy's breath caught. Memories of her original Sassy, the graceful, black beauty who had set out with her on their RV adventure 12 years ago, immediately came to mind. As she aged, her black coat had been overtaken by soft white fur, like powdered sugar sprinkled onto black licorice. Lucy wordlessly hugged Mary close. She closed her eyes but was unable to stop a few tears from escaping between her lids.

"Over here, all you hero dogs, come and get it," Jack tossed a big chunk of cheese to Sassy and Bo each. Boo-Bear timidly approached and took a piece from Jack's outstretched hand. "It looks like you've tamed him well, Mary. He's going to be a fine dog."

Lucy pulled herself together as best she could, then helped Mary clean up from a day and a night in the wilderness. The little group gathered around the fire and finished off the food and water. All agreed: Crackers and cheese had never tasted so fine.

Less than an hour later, two bloodhounds, their handlers, and several sheriff's deputies burst through the undergrowth. Wade and Mr. Davis came up from behind. Wade had talked the officers into letting them tag along.

Everyone was closely inspected and treated for scratches, most of which Jack had tended to the night before. Lucy's limp was from a lightly twisted ankle, which they wrapped securely. Aches and pains resulting from sleeping on the cold, damp earth for a night were just going to have to work themselves out over time.

The return trip was much faster than the zig-zag route they had taken the day before. It turned out they were not far from a national forest trail that connected to the campground trail. Once they reached that, home was only an hour away.

One of the deputies carried Mary, wrapped in the blanket, in his arms. Boo-Bear stuck so closely to his heels that he had to take care not to step on him. Sassy and Bo enjoyed their off-leash time, running circles around the group and teasing the leashed bloodhounds. Lucy traveled more slowly, supported on one side by Jack and by Wade on the other.

Mr. Davis pulled up the rear, pondering the miracle of love and friendship the whole walk home.

Goodbye... Hello

The week had spun full circle. It was Thursday. Both the Davis and Ferguson families were due to leave. Lucy felt relief on the one hand, sadness on the other.

Mr. Davis made a point of coming into the office before he and his family pulled out. Wade was there, reviewing the day's maintenance tasks with Lucy. He was surprised and did his best to suppress a flinch when Mr. Davis approached him, extending his hand.

"Wade, please accept my apology. I fear that I jumped to unpleasant conclusions about you early on. I see now that they were unwarranted. Worse, they reflected badly on myself and all that I believe in. Please forgive me."

Wade took the man's outstretched hand and shook it slowly. He nodded his head, bowed slightly, then walked out the door, his French braid adorned in multicolored, polka-dotted bows swinging behind.

Lucy grinned. "I hope you and your family have a safe journey, Mr. Davis. Please come back to visit again when you are in the area."

"Thank you, Miss Lucy. This campground truly is a wonderful place. I hope the good

Lord will see to our return. In the meantime, please take care of yourself."

He delicately shook Lucy's hand, then made a quick exit. Lucy watched them pull away with their huge rig and sent up a silent prayer for their safety.

A short while later, Mary came running into the office, Boo-Bear leashed by her side. Sassy, who had remained hidden during the previous visit, immediately ran out to greet them.

"Miss Lucy, look how good Boo-Bear is doing walking on the leash! Boy, he is one smart dog, that's for sure, just like my Papaw always said."

"And how is your Me-maw adjusting to life with this little guy in the family?"

"Oh, she likes him just fine. When she thinks we ain't lookin' she sneaks him pieces from her own dinner."

Lucy laughed and bent over to give Mary a big hug. Boo-Bear let her scratch him behind one ear for a brief moment before running off to chase Sassy into the book corner.

Sassy was ready for him.

Hey, squirt, you better take good care of that little girl you caught.

I caught? She caught me, bitch.

Who you callin' bitch?

Who you callin' squirt? Besides, what's wrong with bitch? Ain't that what you are?

Well, yeah, strictly speaking…. Just be sure you show respect for your elders, squirt!

The two dogs tussled good naturedly in the corner. They didn't even notice when Mildred and Henry came in.

"Looks like you got your dog after all," Lucy teased.

"Awww, well, I don't think he'll be that much trouble," Mildred replied. "Mary has stepped up to the plate and is doing all the chores she needs to do to keep him fed and walked and happy."

"Yeah," added Henry. "And when we get back home, I think this little guy is going to make a real good watch dog. He'll keep the coyotes out of the chicken coop and, well, we already know he'll keep a sharp eye on our Mary."

"And that right there counts for everything," Lucy smiled. "I sure hope you can make it back here again. We'd all love to see how everyone is getting on."

"You can bet the ranch on it," Henry assured her.

Hugs were exchanged all around. Henry broke up the dogs' wrestling match then led his little family out the door. Lucy watched Boo-Bear leap after Mary into the back seat of the pick-up truck without any help. He looked like he had already put on a little bit of some much-needed weight.

Her heart deflated a notch when the Fergusons finally pulled out. "Well, girl, I don't know about all the excitement and adventure, but I do know I'm going to miss that sweet family."

Sassy's tail thumped sympathetically.

Yeah, me too. But you know what, Mom? Once those connections are made and that kind of love is shared... I don't think it ever goes away. Somewhere, somehow... something will always remain of it... Even if it is a ghost.

The door jingled and Jack and Bo entered.

"Lucy, Sassy, hello! Think there might be room for us to stay a whole month?"

Lucy leaned across the counter and gave Jack a long, slow kiss. When they came up for air, she slipped back to her computer keyboard and clickety-clacked away. "You're in luck, my dear. And so are we, aren't we Sassy?"

Sassy was too busy covering Bo with sloppy kisses to respond.

* * *

About the Author

Carol Evans and her faithful canine companion (Dawny and, later, Boo) left their routine suburban life behind in 2014 to pursue a childhood dream, joining the ranks of full-time RV travelers. They have met many interesting, wonderful people along the way, many of whom inspire Carol's writing.

Readers are welcome to visit Carol's blog, *Aging on Wheels*: *Where Hell on Wheels Meets Aging in Place (www.agingonwheels.com)*. It has served as both journal and creative outlet. Posts date back to mid-2014, when Carol was preparing to set out on her new adventure.

CAMPGROUND CHRONICLES: SHORT STORIES 1-3, are available individually in ebook format (1st edition), or as a set in ebook or paperback (2nd edition, with minor updates to the individually published stories). All are available through Carol's Amazon Author Page at www.amazon.com/author/carolevans.

THE 30th DAY: A LIFE JOURNEY NOVELLA (Carol's first book) is a work of creative non-fiction crafted around the true story of a very dear friend she met early in her travels. It is also available at her author's page in ebook and paperback versions.

Thank you for reading!